Shakoor Rather is a Kashmiri journalist based in Delhi. He has written extensively about Kashmir's politics, society, culture and heritage. Having grown up in the Kashmir Valley during its most difficult decades, he writes with rare sensitivity about the different dimensions of the conflict there. In a journalistic career spanning nearly a decade, he has also travelled widely, reporting on scientific and technological advancements as well as environmental issues from various countries.

Life in the Clock Tower Valley

SHAKOOR RATHER

SPEAKING
TIGER

SPEAKING TIGER BOOKS LLP
4381/4, Ansari Road, Daryaganj
New Delhi 110002

Published by Speaking Tiger Books in paperback 2021

ISBN: 978-93-89958-84-3
eISBN: 978-93-89958-85-0

10 9 8 7 6 5 4 3 2 1

Typeset in EB Garamond by SÜRYA, New Delhi
Printed at Shree Maitrey Printech Pvt. Ltd., Noida

CONTENTS

1. MATADOR CONFERENCES

SAMAR TRIED TO squeeze his athletic frame onto a shabby, tattered seat right in front of the girl with the red headscarf. She was engrossed in a book, ignoring the pimply boy opposite her who had been staring at her without blinking for at least half an hour. The dilapidated matador finally moved, scattering the rusted chinar leaves on the road and raising a small dust storm. As the pleasant crunching of the dry leaves fell on his ears, Samar heaved a sigh of relief: Finally!

But the relief was short-lived—the matador kept slowing down, often coming to a complete halt every few metres in order to pick up more passengers. On any other day, Samar would have silently waited for the matador to fill up. Today, however, was different. He had to appear for his university semester exams at 11 a.m. Not just that, he also wanted to make an impression on Rabiya, the girl in the red headscarf. He decided to confront the driver. It seemed inconsequential to him that the man was twice his size and had nothing to lose from picking a petty fight.

Samar cleared his throat and with one eye on Rabiya, hollered at the driver, 'Why are you crawling at a snail's pace? Even cyclists and hawkers have left you behind.'

The driver looked up pointedly at the windshield—on which there was a sticker that read 'Driver ko tez chalne par majboor naa karein' (Do not force the driver to drive fast)—before shifting his boorish gaze towards Samar's exaggeratedly angry glare visible in the rear-view mirror. His eyes flashed with an I-don't-give-a-damn attitude, and having failed to get any help from his fellow passengers, Samar was forced to look away from the mirror. As the driver smirked and increased the speed, a tiny, red feather-monkey pasted on the dashboard of the vehicle clapped.

The driver was used to passengers complaining and had learnt to ignore their pleas and threats. He may not have been the owner of the matador, but he was certainly the one whose will would prevail. He would drive or make a stop as he wished. The matador was one of the cramped TATA-407 models with very little legroom and space to stand—made worse by the extra seats the owners had added. Its shabby interior was painted a sickly green and its rusted walls were covered with stickers with Urdu phrases, ranging from sad ones such as 'Qaid mein hai bulbul' (The nightingale is caged) and 'Bewafa se bhi pyaar hota hai' (Love can happen even with the unfaithful); movie names such as *Lucky: No Time for Love*; and religious warnings such as 'Use of amulets and stones is Satan's handiwork'. The air inside had a revolting smell, a mixture of vomit, smoke, unwashed socks and lethally strong ittar.

It was anybody's guess how the transport department allowed these hen-holders-on-wheels to ply on the potholed roads. To make matters worse, drivers would fill them to the brim to earn over and above their daily dues. And when there was no space to stand, people would hang from the doors. Thankfully, such matadors were being phased out in some parts of the state: more comfortable turbo buses were slowly replacing them in Jammu. However, in Srinagar, change seemed a long way away. Owners thought their battered matadors still had life in them, even after having plied on the city roads for over fifteen years. 'A new bus can be put off for another five years at least,' the owners would assure their drivers.

Samar, on the front seat behind the driver, had been quite amazed at his own audacity in challenging the burly driver. His bravery, however, had not yielded the intended results—the driver seemed entirely unperturbed and Rabiya hadn't even looked up. A smile on her face suggested that she had reached an interesting part in the book that she was reading: Gabriel Garcia Marquez's *Love in the Time of Cholera*. Like the book's protagonist, Florentino Ariza, Samar wasn't going to give up on

Rabiya that easily. He tried to impress her again. 'Will you drive faster and stop collecting more people? There is hardly any space in here, soon I'll have to sit in this woman's lap!' Samar shouted at the driver, a little louder this time.

'If you are in such a hurry, why didn't you take an auto?' the driver yelled at Samar.

'Or a plane maybe?' the conductor of the matador joined in. 'Trawunsa yeti—just throw him out.'

This enraged Samar further and he rose and reached for the driver's collar and was about to slap him, when a fellow passenger stopped him. 'He won't listen to you, bhai. Never ever throw a stone in a shit hole.' He said, and turned to buy a pack of peanuts through the window from a nearby vendor.

Samar's face was trembling. 'Kole haenz, bloody fisherman,' he muttered.

As Samar returned to his seat, he realized that Rabiya had chosen this exact moment to turn her attention to the scene. Samar's face turned red. He was mortified that he had lost his cool demeanour at the provocation of that ruffian of a driver. *What will she think of me?* Samar thought as hot, angry tears stung his eyes. This wasn't the kind of impression he wanted to leave on her.

As the driver switched on an Altaf Raja song on the cassette player, the feather-monkey clapped again. 'Ishq aur pyaar ka mazaa lijiye, thoda intezaar ka mazaa lijiye…' (Enjoy the pleasures of love, savour the pleasures of waiting.)

It had taken Samar quite a long time to find out Rabiya's name, and now even a mention of it would make him blush. From the day he had seen her during the university entrance exams, he had hardly been able to take his eyes off her. He knew this was going to be different from his trysts with other women.

Rabiya wasn't just beautiful, she was luminous. Her soulful kohl-smeared eyes were full of grace and mystery. Samar had seen her in the university campus several times. She would always be immersed in a book, sitting in the shade of the thick foliage of one of the lofty chinar trees of Naseem Bagh—the famed Mughal University garden. Her passion for books always amazed Samar. There was hardly a time when she didn't have a book in her hand. He would wonder whether she had made the printed book her veil, with which to shield herself from the real world. He hoped she would notice him if she ever stepped out of that world, which he knew she did because sometimes he would spot her in the company of other girls, sitting in front of the Iqbal Library, or sharing kebabs in the central canteen. Sometimes, Samar would follow her to the recently opened Café Coffee Day, only to watch her sip coffee or eat a spinach sandwich. Any opportunity to see her would make his day brighter.

The Café Coffee Day in the University was one of the few popular restaurant chains in Srinagar. The growing cafe market, a new craze among the youth, was run by locals who gave their shops copy-cat names such as MacDonald, KBC Chicken and Black Bucks. Cafes aimed at college- and school-going youth were opening up in other parts of the city as well, serving the usual pop-western fare of pizzas, pasta, soft drinks and rolls. Some had exciting themes like the magical world of Harry

Potter or the sci-fi universe of *Star Wars*. Many of these cafes were run by optimistic, educated, young men with an entrepreneurial passion, if not aptitude. Most of them had come back from Delhi because they couldn't stand its sweltering, muggy weather. They preferred persevering in the pleasant Kashmir climate rather than finding false comfort in well-paying corporate jobs of the big city.

Samar's train of thought broke when the matador passed by a CRPF bunker, which was enclosed in barbed wire. As always, a helmeted soldier's head peeped out from the turret to keep vigil. Though the University was only a twenty-minute drive from his house, Samar always left an hour earlier to accommodate the snail's pace of the matadors and also the possibility of halts at security checkpoints and bunkers.

After a brief halt at thc bunker, the vehicle gained some speed churning up dust again. But the dusty roads did nothing to obliterate the grandeur of Hari Parbat, a hillock overlooking the city, harbouring the Durrani Fort, which had religious importance for Hindus, Muslims and Sikhs. From

Hari Parbat, the grand old city looked jarring. Its once serene lakes looked like mere canals. The houses seemed like matchboxes stashed compactly next to each other. And the people on the streets looked like ants trying to carry grains through narrow crevices.

As Samar admired the resilience of the fort, his eyes fell upon a spider-web pattern on the windshield of the matador: each thread intricately woven and designed, as if the spider had spent its entire life creating that web. Then a second, more realistic, thought struck him. The pattern had probably been caused by a stone thrown by a protester. Round, rough, small pebbles; bigger, harder-to-grip ones—the protestors used whatever they could find. This stone was probably medium-sized, and might have hit the glass somewhat harmlessly through thick foggy air, damaging the pane a little but not shattering it.

The matador now passed over a wooden bridge on stone pillars that had aged gracelessly and looked resigned to its fate. As Samar pulled out a newspaper from his bag, gory pictures of dead, mutilated faces and rubber-bullet victims sent shivers down his spine. The bag also carried his documents, including his long-due Corporate Law assignments and other notes for last-minute revisions. Just then an old man inquired: 'What's in there, son?'

'What?' Samar initially thought the gentleman was referring to his bag, only to realize that his sunken eyes were on the newspaper.

'Any good news?' the elder asked. Samar paused for a moment, wondering in his head when was the last time he had read something in a newspaper that would qualify as 'good news' and bring a smile to the face of the reader. Curfews, protests, killings, unemployment and corruption were the usual headlines.

Samar handed over his copy of *Greater Kashmir* to the man. He had bought it for a rare old two-rupee note from the vendor at the Sheikh Bagh bus stop where he boarded the matador every morning for the university. He had written his name and phone number on the currency note with a blue-ink pen, before handing it to the vendor. He was hoping it would make its way back to him someday with more names and phone numbers on it.

The gentleman unfolded the newspaper in an orderly way and his face disappeared behind its op-ed page. 'Obama asks India and Pakistan to find a bilateral solution to the vexed Kashmir problem,' the old man read aloud.

A young, clean-shaven man, who was peeping into the newspaper while struggling to stand still in the overfilled matador, chuckled at this. 'Obama or Bush or Clinton, they're all the same, they don't want peace to return. Whatever is happening or has happened in the last two decades is inevitable. Nobody can change the status quo in Kashmir,' he said, turning towards the old person with difficulty amidst the crowd.

Samar nodded in affirmation.

'Kashmir has become a bone of contention between many players now. Only divine intervention can bring back peace and tranquillity to my janate benazeer, my heavenly home,' the young man continued wistfully.

As the matador wobbled to the hub, dust seeped

in through the open spaces. A young woman tried to peer at the newspaper from underneath a man's arm, which gripped the broken handle-pipe on the matador ceiling. The man vehemently objected: she had come too close and was making him uncomfortable. However, on seeing the girl's smiling face, he began to hurl curses at the conductor instead, for filling the matador to the brim. The girl then asked the old man reading the paper to look for any notice about the secondary school exam dates. The man scanned the newspaper carefully until he finally found it. 'Here it is,' he said, turning the paper towards the girl.

'All exams stand postponed due to unavoidable circumstances,' a notice in the bottom left corner of the page read.

As Samar watched through the bunch of heads, he could not guess whether the girl was happy with the announcement or not.

The matador was making rounds of the same area and the conductor was crying out for more passengers, shouting at the top of his voice: 'University, Inversity, yenversity...'

By now the matador had turned into a jumbo circus: nobody knew whose legs were beneath whose bottoms. Meanwhile pages of the newspaper circulated throughout the vehicle, from one hand to another.

Somewhere behind Samar's seat, an argument broke out over an article on the editorial page. Samar turned and craned his neck forward and managed to see a few old black-and-white pictures of Nalah Maar on the page that had caused the argument.

The caption read: 'It's not Venice or Milan; it's Kashmir of yore.'

Nostalgia had stirred some old hearts who were now debating whether the author of the piece had done justice to the stream's lost charm. The old man sitting next to Samar took out a single-filter Four Square cigarette from his pocket and miraculously managed to light it in the crush without setting anyone on fire. As he took long drags from it, he said he was reminded of his first love affair on the banks of Nalah Maar, and how both his love and Nalah Maar had fallen prey to the rust of time.

Nalah Maar was a canal that often found mention in the legends Samar's grandfather told him when he was a little boy growing up in Shehr-e-Khas. It used to run through old Srinagar and connected a lagoon to the famous Dal Lake. The stream was at its best during the reign of the fifteenth-century king of Kashmir, Zain-ul-Abidin, also called 'Budshah'. It was considered to be the city's lifeline. When snow melted at the start of spring, a stream of water would come down from the mountains and drain out through the canal. Nalah Maar protected Srinagar even during the great flood of 1903 while the upper town, including Amira Kadal and other areas, got inundated. The Maar was an important business centre and an easy way of transportation. All vegetables grown in the areas around the Dal lake would be transported through Nalah Maar to people's homes. Samar had seen images from archives that showed tourists flocking the canal with boatmen offering them rides in the crystal-clear waters in doonga boats, floating past rows of Persian-style waterfront houses with flower beds.

The canal was filled up in the 1970s, long before Samar was born, to pave the way for a road through the old city. It had proved to be an ecological disaster for Srinagar, as it choked the lagoon and affected the entire water system of the city.

'How would the Great King react if he saw the Maar today... Or maybe he already knows about the loss and is weeping in his grave!' The old man next to Samar said and sighed.

As the matador drove over what was once the bank of Nalah Maar, the muddy water was visible only in patches—the only reminder of those once aquamarine waters with flowery banks and trout, a paradise for boatmen and their tourists. Amidst the roar of gushing waters, the fishermen would spread their nets to catch a few fish.

But those scenes belonged to a glorious past. Now, orange-feet ducks with dirty beaks could be seen marching on a mission, one following the tail of the other. The canal was choked with weeds, rubble, mossy stones and construction debris. There were carcasses of dead animals and scrawny pye dogs and vultures feasting on them. Everyone in the matador covered their noses for a while and turned their backs to the scene.

The matador stopped at the foot of Hari Parbat, near the shrine of the sixteenth-century Sufi saint Hamza Makhdoom Sahib, popularly known as Makhdoom sahib, Hazrat Sultan or Sultan-ul-Arifeen. The most faithful and resolute devotees climbed its steep, frosted stairs, seeking the blessings of the saint. Outside the shrine, Samar looked at the stone-carvers on the roadside. They were busy working on the stones, making them as smooth as possible. The smoothest among them were meant to be the tombs of the dead. Or of those who had just vanished into thin air: the disappeared of the valley. These were mostly young men whose whereabouts were known to no one, including their parents who would keep a close eye on the door, hoping they would return some day. The wives of these disappeared were called half-widows. People had built symbolic graves for these 'disappeared'—men who, for those who loved them, were unalive, the undead.

Not far from the shrine was the martyr's graveyard, with decades of dead bodies. Here, it seemed as if the dead had reincarnated in narcissus beds.

'Sangtarash—Gpave Yard Stones': this was what was written on a stall, which the stone-workers had temporarily raised on the roadside near the graveyard—and the spelling error went unnoticed. Like every other city, Srinagar too had mistakes on the hoardings all over. The errors reminded Samar of the historical mistakes committed by successive rulers of Kashmir. Like the filling up of Nalah Maar to lay roads rather than reviving the canal.

An old man, with his moustache dyed a pinkish orange, was standing next to Samar. He alighted from the matador at the next stop. While the man patiently waited for the conductor to return his balance money, the conductor continued chatting with the driver. Meanwhile, a few women boarded the matador, as did a person with a grave look on his face, carrying a heavy sack of eatables. He settled in the already over-occupied seat next to Samar. It wasn't long before the fellow removed a cucumber from his bag and took a big bite, the juice spraying all over Samar's face. He did not bother to offer an apology and simply smiled.

Samar took out his handkerchief and wiped his face, stealing a quick glance at Rabiya who was settled comfortably in her seat, still reading.

It was 10 a.m. already. Samar was supposed to report for his test half an hour early, which meant he had to reach within the next half hour. The university was still quite far and Samar would also have to walk all the way from Rumi Gate to reach Naseem Bagh, where the Law Department building was.

As the crowd started easing from the matador, Samar waved at a familiar face that suddenly became visible to him in the crowd. It was his neighbour, Sheikh Mubarak, standing at the other end of the matador. With some difficulty, Mubarak managed to reach the corner where Samar was sitting.

Mubarak ran a metal workshop near Samar's house. He was in the habit of narrating interesting anecdotes from his life to anyone who would listen, even if it meant climbing over his neighbour's wall or boring the customers who came to his workshop. And if there was nobody around, he would send his daughter, Sana, to bring Pintoji, the neighbourhood simpleton.

But on most days, a matador ride gave Mubarak enough opportunities to discuss his life with fellow passengers who were mostly mere acquaintances or even complete strangers. Today he was discussing Sana's prospects of getting admission at a good school.

Meanwhile, Samar was left to pay Mubarak's fare as well: 'Eight plus eight equals sixteen,' Samar told the conductor, who was struggling to calculate. Mubarak shrugged, as if to say, 'I'll pay you later', and continued talking about Sana.

From the story of Sana's birth, Mubarak jumped to another story of how he had acquired his very first set of original Ray-Ban glasses, gifted by a tourist from the Netherlands who had visited his metal shop. Samar had heard the story a million times before and it was torture to have to hear it again. He was hugely relieved when the conductor shouted 'University'. He shot up from his seat.

This was his stop; Rabiya also got up from her seat. She alighted from the matador, pausing at the door to glance at Samar. Samar's head swam and his heart began to hammer against his ribs. She had looked at him! But he had the good sense to get off the matador as if he was in full control of his head and heart, and to walk behind her, carefully maintaining a respectable distance between them.

2. LOVE IN THE TIME OF CURFEW

SAMAR DIDN'T ALWAYS wear a stubble. He used to be clean-shaven, lean and fair. His friends and relatives often called him angrez. When he thought of joining a gym, his friends would mock him by saying that he would vanish if he did so because of his lean build. However, Rauf goor (milkman), a neighborhood shopkeeper who sold confectionary and milk items, inspired Samar to join a gym. Samar would drop by at his decrepit shop on hot summer evenings to savour a glass of buttermilk with choch wor (freshly baked bread). Rauf goor made the tastiest buttermilk in the area. When

Rauf would turn on a tap and let the water flow into a mud pot full of creamy curd and start churning the buttermilk, his biceps would bulge from under the sleeves of his well-worn T-shirt which had a picture of The Rock on the front.

Once when Samar was leaning against an electric pole and enjoying his creamy buttermilk, Rauf, referring to Samar, said to a fellow shopkeeper: 'Bhai has a cute face, great height, and a killer smile. Look at his dimples. But bhai is khataem (wrecked).'

He then turned towards Samar and gave him some unsolicited but friendly advice, 'If you hit the gym, build your biceps and develop your shoulder muscles, girls will kill for you, wallah! By God.'

Samar almost choked on his buttermilk when he heard this but decided to take the advice. Perhaps it would help him impress Rabiya.

The next morning, Samar joined the gym where Rauf worked out, located near the Maharaja-era post office at the extreme end of Sheikh Mohalla. Rauf introduced him to the trainer who doubled as the manager of the gym, and convinced him to enroll Samar for a six-month fitness programme at a discounted fee.

And thus, every morning Samar would wake up to the alarm at 5 a.m., before the first rays of sun made their way into his room, wash his face, gargle with hot water, eat six bananas as recommended by Rauf, and walk to the gym.

'It's always good to warm up before a workout,' Rauf had advised him. Samar wore branded T-shirts and shorts that his brother Adnan had sent for him from Delhi. Adnan would buy branded clothes at throwaway prices at Delhi's Sarojini Nagar Market and the infamous Palika Bazaar, and then either send them over to Samar through courier or carry them with him during his visits to Kashmir for Eid or summer breaks. After a few months at the gym, Samar's hardwork paid off. There was a marked difference in his physique.

As the warm colours of autumn embraced Srinagar's landscape, Samar's infatuation with Rabiya grew stronger. Throughout the year, he would take the same matador back home from the University as Rabiya. On one such airy evening, he walked slowly behind her to the makeshift bus stop at the university gates. Rabiya settled in a tiny rickety seat in the packed matador as Samar stood holding the overhead handrail. Although Samar was tired from the day's activities, standing in the same matador as Rabiya felt much better than sitting in a comfortable seat of a Sumo cab. The conductor kept screaming at him, asking him to move so that he could fill in more people, but Samar ignored him and fixed his shy gaze on Rabiya instead. As the matador started, Rabiya finally seemed to have noticed him. And seeing that he was barely able to stand straight, she turned towards Samar and said, 'Why don't you give your bag to me?'

Samar couldn't believe his ears! She had spoken to *him*. It was as if she had finally acknowledged his existence. He should have just handed over the bag to her, but instead he smiled and said, 'Thank you, I will manage.'

'Are you sure?' Rabiya asked, looking at him with her piercing eyes.

'Yes, it's alright,' said Samar, both excited and

slightly nervous. Rabiya said nothing more and looked out of the window.

As the moment passed, Samar began regretting his lost opportunity.

At the next stop, a man in a canary-yellow Pathani suit boarded the matador and stood next to Samar. The man was carrying a live wild rooster in his bag, and its long neck was protruding from a hole in the bag. Soon enough the rooster started pecking at Samar's bare arm. An irritated Samar freed his hand from the strap he was holding on to, and in the process his bag slipped and dropped into Rabiya's lap. Rabiya looked up and smiled, giving Samar an 'I told you so' look, but all he managed to say was, 'Thank you.'

Just then a frail man on crutches boarded the matador. 'Asalaam-u-Alaikum. Please forgive my interruption,' he began. 'My name is Ghalib and I am homeless. My wife died from cancer a long time ago. And I was crippled by a disease.'

He took out a laminated sheet and showed it to the passengers by lifting it as high as he could stretch his crippled arm. He was struggling to hold the paper with just the three fingers on his right hand. No one bothered to read the words written on that tattered sheet.

'I request you to support me so that I can get my daughters married. There are three of them, all of marriageable age. If you could spare a few rupees, I'd really be grateful and Allah will bestow upon you his mercy and kindness. He will ease your pain, secure your future hereafter.'

Samar pulled out his wallet, and handed over one of the ten-rupee notes to the man, who brushed past him in thankfulness: 'May Allah secure your future. May he bestow you with his biggest rewards, son.'

The man then hobbled from seat to seat collecting some money. But then he suddenly stopped, and looked around to find most people lost in their mobile phones, not acknowledging his existence. And in order to draw attention, he started weeping loudly, and his voice rang through the tiny matador. But the passengers seemed indifferent to his situation. Some giggled uncomfortably. Some pretended he was not there at all. The indifference shocked both Samar and Rabiya, who looked at the man full of sympathy and then towards each other.

'You must know that I don't like asking you for money. I hate living like this. I wish you'd just wonder why my life turned out this way,' the man continued. But before anyone could reply, even in their reluctance, he stopped and then in a mellow voice he continued: 'Keep your money. But please just ask me once how I became this, ask me why I am not like everyone here in the matador. I am begging you, not just for your alms. Please ask. For God's sake only once,' he said while hopping out before the matador could pick up pace.

~

It had been a month since Samar had become acquainted with Rabiya. They would take the same matador to university every day but they hadn't spoken to each other yet. They would mostly just shyly smile at each other. Of late though, Samar hadn't seen Rabiya in the university campus and that made him restless. Every day, he would look for her at the Khanyar bus stop, where she usually embarked on the bus for the university, but was left disheartened each time. Her sudden absence left him confused. He wondered if she had left the university, or perhaps even the city, to study elsewhere. Or was she just suffering from a bout of flu? Sometimes in his desperation, a scarier thought would come to his mind: 'Did she get engaged?' But he would quickly reassure himself by thinking that if that were the case, she wouldn't have bothered speaking to him at all.

When he found himself turning too desperate, Samar often contemplated asking one of Rabiya's classmates, Rifat, about her. However, he deferred acting on it, anticipating that she might find it strange. He also thought Rabiya would probably prefer to keep their friendship a secret.

As the dull week came to an end, Samar couldn't contain his anxiety anymore. When he saw Rifat in the canteen talking to her friends, he decided to ask her about Rabiya.

'Salaam, can you tell me where your friend is? I haven't seen her in the university since last week,' he asked nonchalantly, trying to mask his nervousness.

Rifat smiled. She had been expecting this question from Samar. Rabiya had told her friends about a tall guy she had met in the matador, who studied in the same department and seemed to be interested in her. Looking at Samar's disappointed face, it wasn't difficult to guess that he was the same tall fellow.

'Which friend are you talking about?' Rifat asked Samar, pretending to not know who he was referring to.

'The one who wears a headscarf,' he replied.

'Which one? Many of my friends wear headscarves!' she teased him.

'I know. But I'm asking about the one who has been absent for the last few days. You know who...'

'Why do you want to know?' asked Rifat, extending her little game.

'Can't I ask? It's all right if you don't want to tell me. I just wanted to ask if everything was okay,' Samar said, feeling quite embarrassed.

'You are talking about Rabiya, right?' Rifat asked smilingly.

'Yes! Rabiya...Rabiya. Where is she?' Samar said.

'She is all right. Her sister got married this week. She was busy with the wedding festivities. She will join classes from Monday,' Rifat told him.

Samar thanked Rifat and left in a joyous mood. As he was about to leave, Rifat asked him his name.

'Samar! Samar Mirza,' he said.

'Alright, Mr Samar Mirza, I will tell Rabiya you were looking for her,' Rifat said.

During one of their rides to the university, Samar had overheard Rabiya talking on the phone, complaining about the mobile service in her area to a customer care executive. As she confirmed her phone number to the agent, Samar, while standing next to her, had memorized it.

In the last week, Samar had considered calling the number many times, only to give up the idea. He didn't want to risk his impression on Rabiya. But Samar's interaction with Rifat earlier that morning had given him the clue he was looking for—he was now quite sure that Rabiya was also somewhat interested in him.

So that evening, Samar called Rabiya and introduced himself as the guy from the matador, who was also studying the same course as her at the university, but in a different section. 'I wanted to confirm the timings of the moot court on Monday. I missed the class when it was announced so I thought of checking with you,' Samar said in a quivering voice.

Rabiya wasn't very pleased though. In fact, she was furious, unable to believe how Samar had managed to get her number. She yelled at him for having stalked her. 'Listen, I am not a stalker, I just happened to overhear you in the matador,' Samar said in his defense.

'I understand it may not have been easy for you to ask me for my number, but you could have tried at least,' Rabiya replied. As Samar tried to explain further, Rabiya disconnected the call.

The way things unfolded disturbed Samar and he was determined to make things right with her. He apologized over a text message right away and then in person the next day. Rabiya eventually warmed up to him and they grew to share an easy friendship.

3. BAKERY CONFESSIONS

THE HARSH DAYS of January had set in: foggy days best spent in warm, soft blankets and large quilts. It was the month when one couldn't escape the teeth-chattering cold of chilai kalaan, even when confined indoors. Sipping on hot saffron-kehwa, Samar would sit at home all day on the weekends watching mornings turn into evenings and evenings into nights. It would start to snow soon as it normally did around this time of the year.

In Kashmir, different characters pop up in the streets during different seasons: life-size scarecrows during summers to frighten the unrelenting birds hovering over the paddy fields, and the ceremonial snowmen that delight the neighbourhood children celebrating the much-awaited snowfall. There are also some mythical creatures that figure in the folktales: the yechal, which signifies the onset of the spring, is one of them. It is supposed to possess a broad hood to dutifully shovel and clean up the leftover snow on the streets.

The start of winter always fascinated Pintoji, who lived in Samar's neighbourhood. Pintoji was a twenty-three-year-old stoutly built man with a well-groomed moustache, a clean-shaven, chubby face and big, round eyes. There were days when he looked at the world with the inquisitiveness of a ten-year-old, and on other days, he would show little interest in the world around him. Pintoji was one of the many newborns abandoned for different reasons. He was only a few months old when he was found on the steps leading to Makhdoom Sahib's shrine. Pintoji was lucky to be adopted by the childless Aftab Ahmad, a clerk in the revenue department who lived in Sheikh Mohalla. When

Aftab found him wrapped in a plastic sheet on the shrine's steps, he lifted Pinto in his arms and announced: 'One who has no one has God by his side.' He felt his wish for a child had been granted by Makhdoom Sahib. People who didn't know Pintoji's story would often quip that Aftab must have been a corrupt officer at the revenue department, and that Pintoji's disability was God's way of punishing Aftab.

One winter morning, Samar woke up and stared at the old blue pendulum clock hanging on the newly painted wall. It was eight in the morning. As he tossed from side to side, he felt as if a bug had entered his nightdress and was prickling him under his right arm. He heard a faint sound, which was becoming louder—it was his mother calling out for him. Samar yawned and slowly got off his bed. He looked out of the window and spotted a chinted woodpecker on the walnut tree in Mubarak's backyard. Its beak was frozen but it was pecking relentlessly at the tree.

Samar finally climbed down the steps of the carpeted spiral staircase built from deodar wood, and made his way to the kitchen, where his mother was busy preparing the morning noun chai. This pink salted-tea, a routine affair in Kashmiri households, is drunk with freshly made baker's bread for breakfast.

'Now that you are finally up, go and wash your face first.' His mother said fondly, ruffling the light brown crop of hair on his forehead.

Samar did as he was told and washed up, applying a thick layer of aloe vera gel on his dry, chapped skin at the end. Of late, the winters in Kashmir had started easing up. But the older women and men always talked about how tough it used to be when they were young. People would freeze in the absence of modern facilities such as heaters and geysers, and electricity supply would last only a few hours. German room heaters, kitchen hamam and air conditioners had made life much more comfortable now. Sometimes exaggerated stories of the unrelenting cold of yesteryears also came up only to be refuted by others. He remembered Salem Apa's bizarre story about an extremely cold spell in the valley when people couldn't milk their cows and goats because their teats had frozen—he still didn't know if it was true. Samar dressed himself as well as he could to brave the cold: he put on layers of woolen clothing, a stole, a cap, a long tweed pheran and a pair of special winter socks made of goat leather. He also carried a fire pot underneath his coarse-clothed cloak.

When Samar returned to the kitchen, his mother had finished preparing noun chai. It looked light and tasty as always. As Samar helped his mother transfer the noun chai into a small samovar with red-hot coal emitting its radiance, his mother kept looking at his puffy eyes starved of adequate sleep. 'What, Ma? I have already washed my face! Look, it's still red from all the scrubbing,' Samar exclaimed.

'Your eyes—why are they red? Why do you chat overnight?' his mother complained. 'And the Twitter, the Facebook, whatever?' She left the sentence hanging in the air.

Samar knew his late-night talks with Rabiya were going to come up someday in conversations with his mother, but the timing was unexpected.

It had been hard convincing his parents to let him install the broadband Internet connection. They had certain conditions and he was to follow them: no late-night chats happened to be one of them. The last few weeks, he had spent most nights talking to Rabiya over the phone, and after she slept, stalking her on Facebook. With no good excuse to explain his late-night chats on the Internet, Samar thought it wise to stay quiet. 'And yes, please don't make friends online. Your dad has noticed that you are chatting with people throughout the night,' his mother warned Samar while handing him a bakery basket.

'What's wrong with chatting and making friends online?' Samar was exasperated. He didn't wait for a response, just took the bag and left immediately for the market.

Once he was far from his mother's gaze, Samar took a moment to admire the basket she had given him. It was a veer kani basket, made out of wicker willow, and had been a part of his mother's wedding trousseau. One would never have guessed that it was over twenty years old just by looking at it. With the basket swinging in one hand, Samar started walking towards the nearest baker's shop.

Usually it was Samar's father, Shakeel Mirza, who would be assigned this task. But Mirza, who worked for the Command Area Development Department, was surveying hand-pumps in a remote village, and would not be back till the next day.

The bakery was quite a few streets past their house, right at the edge of Sheikh Mohalla. It had been a while since Samar had ventured into those lanes. The old days of socializing were over. Childhood friends, most of whom had gone out of the state for studies and employment, would catch up with him through social networking sites. Those who were still in Kashmir also preferred to say dua and salaam over the Internet. Visiting each other's houses or meeting up at a shop or in the park was a thing of the past. Catching up over barbeques at Khayam or corn feasts in Makai Park, along the boulevard, on breezy evenings was now an occasional affair. Given the grim security situation in the valley, parents would also encourage children to stay indoors once dusk had set in. Even the Jhelum Bund, which used to be a hub for social gatherings until recently, now wore a deserted look. The bund was famous for the number of shops with names that could momentarily confuse an onlooker: Subhana, the worst, was famous among them. The owners advertised themselves as 'the worst' but with the disclaimer that the customers would agree that they are 'the best' before they left the shop.

As Samar walked out of the main gate of his house, which was rusty enough to be recognized from a distance, he passed by Dr Ali's residential clinic. Dr Ali's nameplate had a big dark cross sign which was an unusual yellow. When the Red Cross Society had raised objections to the red sign being used by doctors and medical establishments, including the pharmacies, all over the country, Dr Ali got a green painted over the red. Now it was a shade that was neither red nor green but an unmissable ochre yellow. The patients had started lining up for their appointment at the clinic, braving the chill of that winter morning.

As Samar marched in his blue duckback boots, he felt a familiar chill go down his spine and his body began to shiver. Muffled up and bitten by cold, he could feel the goosebumps on his skin as they made contact with his thermal inners. Soon he walked past a vast field, which was once a playground. As he passed the wilted rose bed near the streetlight, he saw a broken tubelight hanging from it. The streetlight was precisely at the centre of a three-way junction and was designed to throw light on all three streets at nighttime. As a child, Samar used to play under the dim light even after dusk, when the muezzin would call for the Maghreb prayer in a sonorous tone from the nearby Ahle-Hadees mosque. The call for prayer was still the same, but not the streetlight; it had fallen prey to the snowstorm which had swept the valley a few years ago. The tubelight stayed fused, never replaced since, and the electric connection never restored. He couldn't help but recall his carefree childhood days. Oh! How he played cricket on that lush green well-mowed field, fighting for every single run scored either by him or off him! Not everything about the field was the same now: the rusty railings had been painted green, which was a welcome change because otherwise it was easy to lose sight of them while chasing a ball. Samar could still feel the faded scars on his arms from those night-long cricket matches.

In that short saunter to the bakery, Samar came across abandoned shoes, outdated newspapers, old socks, all frozen because of the ice-cold weather. The items seemed so enchanting and deliberately placed that any exhibitor would envy the installation. On one of the newspapers he spotted a few bold, red letters, which read 'Eighteen-year-old killed by Internet friend'. The story was about a teenager who happened to murder a boy his own age because they both liked the same girl. The red ink had grown a shade darker under a thick colourless film of ice. Samar wondered what his mom would have to say about this and his newfound love for Rabiya. He knew that she would feel vindicated on her stand about Internet-friends.

Samar finally reached Nader's Bakery. The bakery's name was written with charcoal on the empty municipality dustbin. A heap of garbage had piled up just a metre away from it. Not very far were the crows picking ticks from the dung-laden backs of stray cows. People had gathered in front of the shop and were waiting their turn to collect bread. Some even carried kangris to fill them with burning coal from the baker's tandoor. It was a long queue; Samar realized it would take some time before his turn came. Through the crowd of people Samar spotted the balding baker smiling at his customers, showing off his blackened teeth. He could vaguely see the baker's paunch, which came to his aid as he worked on the dough: it would press the dough on one side as he would pull the loaf on the other side to give the lavaas its round shape. The baker had lived a hard life but was generous and always put a free loaf in the baskets of his regular customers.

With the cold getting the better of him, Samar sat down on the seat made of rubber tyres. He waved at the baker through the crowd of people, indicating that he would be waiting at by the seating area.

The age-old bakeries, or kandurwaans, in every corner of the city and elsewhere in the valley, were irreplaceable as almost all households depended on them for their bread. The dough is left to ferment overnight and baked into fresh breads and pastries in the morning. The bakers prepare different varieties of breads. The lavaas and girde for breakfast; the fresh til vor or choch vor—a bagel-like bread with poppy seeds, to be smeared with butter or ghee and eaten with the afternoon tea; and crispy bakirkhaen and crunchy kulche to be had with the evening tea.

By now, the bakery had become a centre of discussion where the young as well as the elderly had gathered. Some people were discussing the possible formation of a government by a national party. Which state party was it going to align with was the central question. Another group was discussing the implementation of the Pay Commission for employees: 'If other states have already implemented it, why can't our government follow suit?' Someone was saying angrily. Perhaps everything from Srinagar to Los Angeles, Omar to Obama, Guantanamo bay to Gaza, was being discussed there. These kandurwaans have been one exception in Kashmir's fragile situation. They have always made bread available irrespective of the situation.

These meetings on roads and shops, including at Nader's Bakery, are the 'thought schools of Kashmir', not quite like those elsewhere around the globe. They are the public spheres of the valley. These gatherings witness moments where governments are elected and also elections are won without pressing the ballot button. They offer solutions for every possible problem at hand—from unemployment to terrorism and tourism; from the Kashmir issue to disputes over water treaties.

'Why isn't anybody listening to these ready-made solutions?' Samar would always wonder.

Soon, the baker called out Samar's name; his breadbasket was ready.

On his way back home, Samar saw that the landscape around him had changed. The ice path was quickly turning into a small stream of flowing water. The vehicles passing through the streets had left tyre marks all over. Faint sunrays crept through the clouds like the yolk of an egg seeping out of the dense egg white, and lit up the landscape.

As soon as Samar reached home, he left the breadbasket in the kitchen and hurried to leave for the university.

4. LIONS AND LAMBS

LOCATED IN THE heart of downtown Srinagar or Shehr-e-khaas, Sheikh Mohalla carried the fragrance of yore. The mohalla was representative of a typical Kashmiri neighbourhood. People were helpful, caring. It was like a large family, where the members would just live in separate houses but share almost everything. Doors remained open at all times; kitchens would welcome any hungry soul.

Strategically situated in the shape of an arc around the tomb of Zain-ul-Abidin's mother, Sheikh Mohalla was filled with old Persian-style, beautiful but cramped houses like the one Samar's grandfather had constructed in the early 1970s. Over the years, Samar's father, Shakeel Mirza, had renovated the house from time to time. He even got the base of the building strengthened using cement, iron panels and crushed sand.

The houses in the mohalla were made out of thin, tile-like mud bricks fortified with wooden support panels and had corrugated tin roofs. Doors were made out of framed woodwork and windows were latticed. The insides had filigreed embroidery walls. The most distinct feature of the houses was the quintessential wooden balcony or daeb, which the residents used to enjoy the sunshine, preserve vegetables and dry clothes during the winters, but most importantly to keep an eye on the goings-on of the mohalla. Some of the houses even had tiny wooden bridges connecting the top floors. Bylanes of the mohalla, covered in big cobblestones, were mostly narrow, except for the main road leading to the tomb which was wider than the rest. The narrow roads had small, uncovered sewer-lines running on both sides. Small house gardens were scattered all over, and the usual grapevines, Kashmiri wild roses, tiny pomegranate plants and occasional walnut trees grew in them. The main road had a lane of shops, mostly wholesale distributors of fabric and hardware. Shops selling ropes, kitchen utensils, wood turnery and metal workshops were also a common sight.

But most importantly, everyone in the neighbourhood had clear political allegiances. Samar's father Shakeel Mirza, like his father Waheed Mirza, openly vowed his allegiance to the ruling National People's party. He believed the late Sheikh was the tallest leader the state had ever had. He had even fallen out with many childhood friends who detested him for openly supporting the party and its late leader. A rational and clear-sighted Shakeel would argue about how it was the Sheikh who had liberated the people of the valley from years of tyranny and subjugation under the Maharaja's rule, brought about land reforms, and restored the land-to-the-tiller policy. They were proud 'Sher', as the followers of the Sheikh came to be known. Because his family were Shers, Samar was also considered to be one even though he never associated with either of the groups.

This had invited wrath from many people, especially the Bakras, the supporters of the then Mirwaiz or Chief Priest of the biggest mosque in Kashmir. The joke was that they were called Bakras because of their long flowing beards. They denounced the Sheikh as a traitor who sold their nation for his own political ambitions. He and his party were, for them, the sole reason for the miseries of the people.

The Sher-Bakra rivalry had become a sore point in Kashmiri politics decades before the onset of militancy and continued in some families for generations. In the past, at the peak of the Sher-Bakra fueds, people would often be asked where their loyalties lay—were they a Sher or a Bakra? There would be immense disappointment and surprise if someone were to say 'neither', and fear when encountering a supporter of the opposite side. There were more Shers than Bakras in downtown earlier, but over the years Bakras had taken over. Both groups preferred living in separate areas, clearly demarcated by flags and graffiti. If either were to enter the other area, there was a good chance they would be roughed up.

Although the fierce Sher-Bakra rivalry was a thing of the past, legend has it that once a person from the nomadic community was on a visit to the super-specialty hospital Sher-e-Kashmir Institute of Medical Sciences in Soura. As he ventured through downtown, he was stopped by a group of people who asked him whether he was a Sher or a Bakra. He gave it some thought before pompously announcing that he was a Sher. 'A nomad is always a lion. We rear bakras in flocks, sell them wherever we go, milk them and have dogs to take care of them,' he told the group, who thrashed him and hurled abuses at him. He had to run for his life.

The nomad, according to the tale, stopped by a house to ask for water. As he was sipping water, the head of the family asked him about his condition. 'Some people mistook me for a Sher. Who would ever call oneself a Sher? Is that something to be proud of?' he replied.

'So you are a Bakra,' the head said. To which

he proudly replied, 'Yes janaab, hundred per cent Bakra, I have lived my entire life with bakras. I am a bakra, even my beard is long like a bakra.' The poor man had only just finished sipping his water when some young men from the family threw him out of the house and showed him the way out of the area. The nomad didn't look back till he reached the outskirts of the city. It was only when he saw familiar trees and rice fields and a horde of bakarwaals attending their herd that he breathed a sigh of relief. He then declared that the next time someone asked him whether he was a Bakra or a Sher, he would say: 'Neither Bakra, nor Sher, I am a bastard.'

Samar was smiling to himself thinking of the poor nomad's plight as he boarded the matador that would take him to the university. He found an empty seat and stretched out a leg on to the next seat, saving it for Rabiya. When the men who were standing objected, he argued that he had injured his leg, and needed the extra space. He even offered the conductor the fare for the extra seat, which he accepted. Everybody in the over-crowded matador was muttering curses at him under their breath. Samar quickly texted Rabiya the matador number so that she could get into the same one.

When Rabiya finally boarded the matador, Samar removed his leg from the seat and, acutely aware of everybody's eyes on him, offered the seat to Rabiya. This caused an elderly woman, who had been standing all along, to curse: 'Look, this son of mine has no shame. The world has come to this now.'

'He had to reserve it for this girl. He has no fear of God. Doomsday is near!' another woman nodded in agreement.

But so smitten was Samar that Rabiya was all he believed in and thought about. With her long face, high cheeckbones, the heady fragrance of her hair and her iridescent eyes, she was no less than an Egyptian Goddess to him. He couldn't help but start humming 'Afreen Afreen' every time he saw her, a song he was as obsessed with as he was with Rabiya.

Rabiya was surprised that Samar had reserved the seat for her. By now she knew Samar was head over heels in love with her, but she didn't want him to take anything for granted.

As the matador went along the bumpy roads, Samar's journey of desire began. All of a sudden, he started liking the pot-holed roads; it felt as if he was sitting in a beautiful caravan that was taking him beyond the obvious and the mundane. He no longer complained about the speed of the matador as it gave him more time to spend with Rabiya.

They were now friendly and comfortable around each other. Rabiya didn't even mind Samar's occasional touch. Earlier, their talks had been limited to a customary hello or chats about corporate law classes. But after they started talking on the phone, pretending to ask each other questions about university and their course, they had started becoming more comfortable around each other.

As the summer of Rabiya and Samar's friendship approached, vacations of fifteen days were announced in the university in the midst of another cycle of violence, killings, protests and shutdowns.

5. THE LOST COW

'Saeri samha:v aeksi razi lamh:av,
Telma rawyeh:a kahan g:aav'
(Had all the eleven pulled on their rope,
their cow wouldn't have gone astray)

IT WAS AUGUST. Wet green moss had already settled on the moist ivy brick walls of Sheikh Mubarak's house, engulfing it like a monster about to tear its prey into pieces. A week had passed since the indefinite curfew had been imposed following the ruling coalition government's collapse over protests against transferring acres of forest land to a Shrine Board. Governor's rule had been invoked. Life was paralyzed in every way.

Restrictions had been imposed on peoples' movement. Businesses, schools and shops remained shut. It was time for people to spend days indoors. This unwanted pause from daily routine, however, was a blessing in disguise for some. They used the time to complete pending household work: paint shabby walls and fix plumbing and electric switches. Others, mostly young people, would sulk inside their houses because they could not meet their girlfriends or boyfriends. Samar spent the time talking on the phone with Rabiya. They would wait for the intermittent breaks in the curfew to sneak a quick meeting with each other. Normally, under curfew, Internet services would be curtailed or completely snapped by the government, forcing people to indulge in long discussions face to face. These would be mostly political debates, which would invariably end up in fights over petty issues and difference of opinions. People would take longer afternoon naps, waking up to the same faces around them, and watching one's partner and kids for hours could become unbearably frustrating for most.

Uncertainty was ticking on Mubarak's silver-plated wristwatch placed on his right hand. A flock of crows was circling the sky over the dark pines. An Alsatian dog was chasing the moon somewhere, running across the far-off rice fields. Its bark pierced through the quiet of the night. In the pleasant breeze carrying the whispers of autumn, Mubarak's cow was pregnant. The time of delivery was around the corner. It could be any moment now. Mubarak feared that in case of some complication, he may not be able to convince the vet to visit amidst the curfew. The vet was also an old friend of the family and lived in the adjacent Khan Mohalla. Although Mubarak had informed him about the situation just an hour ago, he dialled the vet's number once again. It wouldn't hurt to remind him, Mubarak thought. To his despair, the phone services had been snapped without notice.

Nestled in the warmth of her mother's lap, Sana, Mubarak's five-year-old daughter, threw a volley of questions at her worried father. 'When is the little one expected to arrive?' she asked curiously. She had heard him telling the neighbours earlier in the evening that the cow was ready to give birth.

'By the time you wake up in the morning, jigar,' was Mubarak's optimistic answer.

'I won't sleep, Abba. I want to be the first one to see the calf,' Sana said, brushing her dark, long curls away from her forehead. She half expected her father to reprimand her. He was always making sure she slept on time. But when Mubarak did not respond, Sana took his silence as permission to stay up late and happily snuggled closer to her mother in the glow of the lantern as shadows of trees outside flickered across their airy drawing room.

Mubarak looked at his daughter. She had inherited his straight nose and her mother's full pink lips. Sana was excitedly telling her mother about how she would play with the newborn calf under the morning sun; perhaps bathe it under the hand-pump in the backyard, in the shade of the walnut tree. Mubarak wished all members of the household would share Sana's enthusiasm. His wife, in particular, had not mentioned the cow's impending delivery even once. It was as if she was deliberately avoiding the subject. Perhaps she did not want to jinx it by talking about it; Naziya could be very superstitious when she wanted something badly, thought Mubarak.

Mubarak could hear the pattering of walnut kernels on the tin roof of Sheikh Manzil. The sound of the falling walnuts at night would often wake Mubarak up in the fear that a thief was trying to sneak into the adjacent metal workshop. The pattering would continue for nearly a month until the walnuts were ripe enough to be harvested. Then the tree branches would lift and recuperate from the stress of bearing the weight of the fruit. During walnut season, the fruits and twigs from the tree, along with the heavy bent branches, would damage the roof of Mubarak's house. Mubarak often considered felling the tree. However, he had developed a certain respect for its stature and age. He valued the benefits it had lent to the Sheikh family over the years; and thus, never acted upon the idea.

Sana went off to sleep that interminable night dreaming about the coming of a friend. Just before she fell asleep, Sana was thinking if she should replace Pintoji, her current playmate, with the calf. Mubarak held her slender frame in his arms and carried her to the bedroom upstairs. He laid her down and watched her sanguine face rest comfortably on the fluffy pillow.

And then Mubarak went downstairs to look for his wife. Now that Sana was asleep, they could discuss what needed to be done to ensure that their cow gave birth smoothly. But this was not the only reason Mubarak wanted to talk about the cow to his wife. He did not like to admit it, but he was scared, and he needed to speak about his fears; hear some words of comfort and hope, in response.

But his fears were not to be assuaged. Naziya was fast asleep. Mubarak wondered if she was pretending. Afterall, she had been sitting up just a few minutes ago but now she seemed to have drifted to another land. Her pheran had ridden high up her legs, exposing her thin, wobbly knees. Mubarak felt a wave of desire for his wife. He wanted to hold her, kiss her, bury his head in her bosom and forget his troubles. He stroked her hair but she did not stir. Mubarak at once felt tired and exhausted. He slumped down next to her on the floor, and waited through the dubious night for the curfew to be relaxed.

It would be relaxed at 8 o'clock in the morning for an hour. This was when people could add to their stocks of rice, wheat flour, baby food, oil, medicines and other essentials. If nothing untoward happened during that hour, the authorities sometimes extended the relaxation—Mubarak consoled himself with the thought. He was intently listening to his vintage Phillips Bahadur transistor, which was wrapped in a black leather cover and eternally placed on the windowsill of the dining room. To Mubarak, it seemed the radio and Naziya were alike: they worked perfectly well throughout the day, but often tuned out during the most important parts.

Mubarak paced the room as the morning sun greeted him from across the window. A streak of orange fell on the wall, lighting up the dust particles on its way, like a movie being projected on a screen. He stopped to look at his shadow on the wall. He looked much thinner than he actually was.

Then he turned his attention back to the cow. The time of the cow's delivery was drawing near. Mubarak had seen the tell-tale signs exhibited by the cow. To compound the inconvenience caused by the curfew, there had been a shortage of milk in the valley for over a month. Days had gone by with black salt-tea for the family. Black tea in white cups, half-sips gulped down half-heartedly.

Exactly at fifteen past eight in the morning, the vet showed up at the door in an army-green jacket with wool scrapings coming out of the burnt hole in his collar at the back. He wore long hippy trousers and was carrying a white cowboy hat pressed tightly under his arm. People referred to him variously as Dactor Saeb, Doctor Sahab, Gupan Dactar (animal doctor) or 'vetanary'. He was carrying his equipment in a brown Gucci leather satchel, courtesy the Sunday flea market. He would often be seen carrying two things on his person: his second-hand bag and his first-hand notion of being the only professional around. Once in a while, he would even examine humans and prescribe medicines. Mubarak rushed him to the backyard where the cow was.

Hearing the commotion, Sana woke up and ran towards the window facing the backyard. She peeped through the windowpane to look into the cowshed, her pink cheeks and green eyes pressed against the mesh of the window. She looked like a daffodil flowering under the sun, emerging from the mud pot, growing tall against gravity. She greeted the vet with a salaam, but he barely noticed. He was already busy examining the cow, not wanting to waste any more crucial time.

Sana's mother had found herself something to do in the balcony enclosed with pinjra jaalis, on the second floor of the house. Naziya was trying to distract herself from the happenings around her. She was wearing a brown cotton pheran with qurab sleeves folded back, and with silver embroidery all over the chest and the edges. The small wrinkles around the corner of her eyes, belying her age, had stories to tell; perhaps the sorrow of not being able to conceive a child for a long time had made them deeper. The cow had been a favourite of her mother-in-law. When she was alive, she never allowed Naziya around the cow. Once when her mother-in-law was unwell, Naziya had gone to milk the cow. The cow wasn't comfortable around her and kicked whenever she came near her. But that didn't mean Naziya hated the cow or didn't want it to do well through its labour—she was just indifferent.

She watched Sana through the colourful translucent glass window that had aged and melted in summer afternoons over the years. Trusses of red chilies hung from the wooden nail on the brick wall to bake in the sun, and sliced bottle gourds and brinjals were kept in a cane tray to dry.

While the vet examined the cow, Mubarak looked on with helplessness on his face and hope in his heart. The varied shapes and sheen of the tools the vet was carrying seized his attention. For a few seconds, Mubarak's mind was mired in thoughts of his metal workshop that continued to bear the brunt of indefinite curfews and strikes. He had never had the opportunity to use so many tools in the metal workshop.

Mubarak's train of thoughts was interrupted by the vet's urgent voice. The cow had developed complications. He quickly wrote down a prescription. 'Get these hormone injections. They are necessary for your cow. Get them at any cost,' the vet was speaking to him.

A troubled Mubarak thought of his childhood when no such complications would arise. Cows delivered without any hassle. All they needed was someone to look after them. No such procedures were followed, for one life to survive and for another to arrive. Mubarak didn't know how to get the injections in the curfew and neither did the doctor. He himself had run out of supplies.

As if on a mission, Mubarak leaped and howled through the street, running breathlessly towards the market to find a veterinary medical shop. At the end of the street he encountered a barricade erected by the cops.

The potholes were big enough to harbour colonies of shelled molluscs during rains. Mubarak looked up towards the sky: dark clouds were fast appearing over his head. He felt that God had shut all doors of kindness on the Sheikh family. He ran through the opposite street, looking for a medical store there, but in vain. Mubarak stood helpless against the backdrop of the brick wall where the graffiti read, 'Sheikh the Messiah, Sheikh the traitor'.

Mubarak passed by Dr Ali's residential clinic. The shutters were down. He approached the alley leading to the main door of Dr Ali's house only to be greeted by a metal lock on the door.

Where could he be, Mubarak wondered. Just last week, he had heard at the bakery about an anonymous letter addressed to the doctor. Maybe he had left the valley like other renowned practitioners, who had gone to other countries seeking peace and better opportunities. Or could it just be a family vacation?

As a dejected Mubarak traced his steps back towards the street, his eyes fell on the hoardings hanging on the electricity poles on the roadside near Hamza mosque. A flock of pigeons sat in a straight line on the wires, as if they had been lined up for a military crackdown. They took turns to fly to the ground to peck on corn and rice grains thrown for them. Sprinkled with bird droppings, some of the electricity poles had turned grey and white. One of the hoardings put up by the electronic giant LG read 'Life's good'. The irony of the situation was not lost on Mubarak. He had made every effort to get the injection to save his cow, even climbing walls to ask for it from people who he knew had cows. A few chemists who had opened their shops turned him away as they did not have it and some others were rushing to lower their shutters as the deadline for the reimposition of curfew was nearing.

Vultures had gathered over the skies of Sheikh Mohalla when he reached his house. He rang the doorbell with trembling hands and the grim, mournful face of his wife appeared. As the vultures took their positions on the sky-high poplar trees, Mubarak turned pale. His heart began to race as if he had run a marathon. The cow had been more than an animal, worth more than the seven thousand rupees it was bought for, more than the milk and curd she gave. All the tools of the doctor and all injections were irrelevant now. The curfew had sucked out his hope and his cow's life.

He walked to the cowshed where he saw Sana point at a movement in the straw. A souvenir left by the cow rested on the ground—all covered with gum and hay, like a crimson strawberry topping on a vanila ice cream. The cow had delivered. Sana was jubilant, but sensing the grief on her father's face, she decided not to smile. Looking at the carcass on the patch of hay right next to the calf, Sana quietly asked her father, 'What will happen now, Abbu?'

'Black tea for a few more months, Sana,' Mubarak replied with a wry smile.

Amidst this hustle, I seek thou
In profound suffering this feeling somehow
How easy it seems, but to say goodbye
I'll measure your return through the arch of my bow
I tried and destiny had a tale to tell
I pray for your journey my dear cow
My cow, my lost cow.

6. A WALK IN THE CLOUDS

SAMAR HAD BEEN waiting for the brief holiday period to end and the situation to improve, so that he could meet Rabiya again and walk with her under the shade of the chinar trees. For Samar, love seemed to engulf him whenever he walked down the university corridors with Rabiya. How beautiful that place had become for Samar. Life was good when Rabiya was around. Rabiya blushed every time Samar looked at her face.

Finally one morning after the curfew was lifted, Samar boarded the matador and, as always, reserved a seat for Rabiya. When Rabiya boarded the matador, Samar offered her the seat and she settled down next to him. Rabiya's delicate hands moved nimbly. To Samar's surprise, she dropped a bag onto his lap. He could see some gifts through the translucent white-and-red bag.

'What is in there?' Samar asked with a child-like restlessness. Several unrelated thoughts crossed his mind.

'Open the bag later at home,' a shy Rabiya whispered in Samar's ear.

More than the gifts, Samar was thrilled by the fact that Rabiya had taken the moment to come closer to him. He could feel the warmth of her body, and the warm air from her mouth that had touched his ears. As he held her hand tightly in his, Samar's heart began to race and his head spun.

Just then a young man, who had been staring at them for some time, made his way past the crowd and approached them. He slapped Samar. Before they could process what had just happened, the man started hurling abuses at them. A furious Rabiya snapped back, but the man screamed at her: 'Sit down, you shameless whore! It's because of girls like you, Kashmir is facing this situation.' This infuriated an already shocked Samar and he grabbed the man by his collar and got into a fistfight with him.

The conductor and the driver of the bus, with the help of a few passengers, separated the two and showed the young man out of the matador. As Rabiya tried to pacify Samar, some people, including women, could be heard justifying the actions of that man.

After that unsavoury incident, Samar started driving his father's car to the university. Shekel Mirza hardly used it so it had been a mere showpiece at the Mirza House. But Samar couldn't simply pick up Rabiya from her neighbourhood. So she would take the usual matador from her stop every day and get down at the next stop, where Samar would be waiting for her.

~

Rabiya had obliged her parents by complying with religious rituals. When she had first seen Samar in the university, she had no interest in him. But over time, she started liking him. Little things, like his caring nature and his ever-smiling face had won her over. When Samar finally asked her out for a date, she went without informing her friends or parents. She agreed to meet him in a dimly lit restaurant located on the second floor of a small shopping mall near Lambert Lane. She was nervous, and so was Samar. They both kept looking around for a possible relative or a neighbour or some acquaintance they might bump into.

Samar and Rabiya weren't just compatible when it came to their career choices or their similar worldviews, they would even complete each other's sentences. 'Great people always think alike,' Samar joked, whenever they talked about the most important issues in their lives. Their relationship had started growing and they felt they were perfect for each other.

On a short trip organized by some friends from the university, Samar and Rabiya visited the Burzahom archeological site, not very far from the university campus. Burzahom was the first Neolithic site to be discovered in Kashmir, located between the banks of the Dal lake and the Zabarvan hills, about five kilometres from the famous Mughal Garden of Shalimar. Samar and Rabiya managed to split from the rest of the group and found a secluded place. Behind the ancient cave mounds, Samar and Rabiya kissed for the first time. Rabiya was slightly hesitant and unsure of how to act in the spur of the moment but eventually pulled him closer in a tight embrace as the Himalayan bulbuls looked on. The kiss, and the emotions surrounding that intimacy, were so potent that their rapid heartbeats were audible amidst the cooing of mating pigeons and the chirping of cicadas. It was a special moment, one that neither was going to forget anytime soon.

7. THE COMPULSIVE MATCHMAKER

SANA HAPPENED TO come late into Mubarak's life. As Mubarak's wife Naziya had developed complications during her first pregnancy—which had to be terminated—some doctors had ruled out any chances of her conceiving in the future. The Sheikhs even thought about adopting a child from Yateem Trust.

The orphanage had several hundred children waiting for adoption. People would generously donate to the Trust, which sent tiny vans playing emotional songs, mostly sung by children at a high pitch, through the nooks and corners of the city and districts elsewhere. The songs hit an emotional chord with the people who would reciprocate with whatever means they had. Some donated old clothes, others gave cash. Only a few would actually adopt the children.

The family, however, gave up on the idea of adoption when Salem Apa, an elderly woman from the neighbourhood, came up with the prospect of visiting a revered dervish, who lived in some far-off village. With her impressive persuasive abilities, she cajoled the couple into visiting the pir in the forest land.

Salem Apa sold aabe-hayaat, the water of immortality, to others while she herself was standing at the edge of her grave. Why doesn't she drink it herself, people would wonder. Salem Apa was in her fifties but her resolute face didn't give away her actual age. She was fond of wearing bright-coloured chinted pherans with qurab sleeves and tila embroidery all over, which she complemented with contrasting pyjamas. She still washed her hair with shikakai in the hope of turning her aged white hair back to black, and gulped down Vasmol tablets as a quick colouring-fix. She had slanted eyes on which she applied a thin line of soorma from a copper shishi. Once a week she would treat her hair with a mixture made by dissolving seem aab (tiny balls of mercury) in mustard oil to achieve long, bouncy tresses. She fed herself a special diet consisting of two full meals a day that contained rice and minced meat cooked in mustard oil. Although her income didn't allow her to splurge, she would not compromise on her nutritious diet. She only cooked food in the mustard oil milled through a water machine, even if that meant walking to the suburbs of the city to an old mill where turbines would run with the strong current of water falling from a height. She didn't like the food processed at power mills, saying it was not only costly but also too hot for the body; that it gave her stomach ulcers and heartaches. Her special masalas were ground only with a wooden muhul (pestle) in a traditional kanz (mortar) made of deevar stones at her rented house near Sheikh Mohalla. She gorged on homemade curd and safed noun chai three times a day. She prayed five times a day, describing those who only offered the fajr (morning) and asar (evening) namaaz as pretentious and turncoats.

Salem Apa was originally from a village in the Anantnag town of south Kashmir. She had been married to Asrar Khan of Shahr-e-Khaas, who had been disinherited for marrying a village girl. After his death in an accident, Salem Apa and her son Sartaj were turned away by her mother-in-law. Since Salem Apa didn't have any other means to survive and support herself and her son, she rented a room in Sheikh Mohalla and took to matchmaking, which was a lucrative profession in Kashmir. During her younger days, she would neatly pack lunch for her son and send him to a government school every morning, then leave with a cloth satchel, hunting for prospective grooms and brides.

Her profession demanded that she travel the length and breadth of the city and other far-off places in the valley. Initially she had restricted her dealings to the city, but later on when her son was older, she expanded to other districts. Given her familiarity with south Kashmir, she found clients with ease. She knew how many kids were there in a family. She could pass off as a repository for childbirth registration. Over the years she earned enough money to build a small two-bedroom house in the outskirts of the city, where she was delaying shifting due to the compulsion of her work. She would work in unique ways and keep track of people approaching marriageable age. She took due care of class and caste demarcations. Families of Syeds and Bukharis would always look for a match in their extended peer clan as they considered themselves to be the direct descendants of the Prophet and therefore at the top of the societal hierarchy. Proposals from Sheikhs and other such castes would be frowned upon by them. Dhars, Bhats, Rainas and others were not acceptable, given that at some point in the history, their ancestors had converted to Islam.

Salem Apa had been instrumental in arranging Mubarak's marriage with Naziya, but the nuptial knot had proven a difficult one, both for Salem

Apa as well as for Naziya, who wasn't able to bear a child for a long time into her marriage. Her mother-in- law made life difficult for Naziya, taunting her all the time. She even nursed a grudge against Salem Apa for bringing Naziya's marriage proposal to Sheikh Manzil. Naziya started hearing veiled jibes and insinuations in the most innocent comments. Naturally, Salem Apa felt empathetic towards Naziya and hoped to help her in whichever way possible.

8. THE BLESSED ALMOND

FINALLY, A YEAR after Naziya's mother-in-law had passed away, Salem Apa got a chance to help Naziya. On Salem Apa's insistence six years ago, in the hours before dawn could set in, she left for Safed Gul with Mubarak and Naziya. It was a small hamlet in south Kashmir where a revered dervish lived and practiced. Mubarak wondered if the dervish was some wanted fugitive or a counter-insurgent or a renegade working for the government, disguised as a godman. Probably that was why he was hiding in the woods, behind thorns and stones, away from the worldly gaze.

After travelling for the most part of the hot sunny June morning, through a mountainous terrain and thickets of forest, they reached a place with big marble-white rocks. On their way they had crossed the vast saffron and rice fields, willow nurseries and poplar groves; and the bat-manufacturing industries on both sides of the national highway, with bats and posters of cricketers from around the world on display. They halted at Anantnag town for a quick tea break before setting off again for Safed Gul.

On their way from Anantnag, they had to halt for a security check. At the checkpost everybody got down from the vehicle and walked in a straight line, flashing their identity cards high up in the air. They conducted themselves in the best possible manner without showing any visible signs of fear, and avoided the ever-suspicious eyes of the gun-toting soldiers in army fatigues. Most commuters were used to the checking; they remained normal and acted as if it was any other routine chore. But for Mubarak, this was an insult. He disliked the idea of having to prove his identity every time, in his own land—his land of chinar trees and snow-capped mountains.

They reached the small hamlet amidst the chirping of cicadas overlaid with the chatter of the crows—and the marching tune of soldiers in the nearby army camp, known to serve as one of the biggest ammunition depots for the army in the state. It was another world altogether.

As the trio approached the village, Mubarak saw a handful of houses carved out of stone and deodar wood scattered amidst the wild greenery. The cramped stone houses, quite unlike the houses in the valley, butted against each other. It seemed as if that place had run out of land stock. Mubarak was sullen and tired from a long hot day's journey and Salem Apa's outlandish stories about the dervish's healing powers.

While Mubarak and Naziya yawned and cursed the potholed dusty road leading to the village, Salem Apa enjoyed the fresh aroma of deodar trees with their ripe cones strewn over the roads.

She took off her shoes to feel the soothing grass meadow near the glacial stream.

'This air rejuvenates my soul. It's not for nothing that Kashmir is called Heaven on Earth,' she said, while prostrating for zuhr prayers under the shade of an apple tree.

As the village came into view, Mubarak tried to guess which one was the dervish's house. 'I think the one with green windows,' said Naziya.

'No, that's too small for a dervish. Maybe the one near those loudspeakers?' he replied.

'It looks like a mosque,' Naziya said.

'Yes, definitely the one near the mosque. What do you think?' he asked Salem Apa.

Both Salem Apa and Naziya put up their hands in front of their eyes to block the piercing sunlight and simply nodded in assent. The village was known as Safed Gul to the locals and even to the pathwari who had very few records to handle in a hilly terrain. It was afternoon and their shadows had started growing longer with the vast blue sky and bright orange sun overhead.

'Its name is Safed Gul owing to the abundance of white rocks around this place,' Mubarak whispered in Naziya's ear.

'Oh! Is that the case? But what about Gul? There are no flowers around here,' she asked inquisitively.

Mubarak didn't have any answer to that, so he brushed her off and said in an irritated tone: 'Just follow me. You women have no sense of direction.' In the official records of the nearby tehsil office, however, Safed Gul was called Safed Deva.

A discrepancy which even Mubarak acknowledged while reading one of the milestones on the way.

There was confusion over names of several places in the valley. Some would use the ancient and more locally popular names, while others would settle for the modern official usage. Islambad in south Kashmir had become Anantnag—probably because of it being a namesake of the capital of Pakistan. Likewise, Varmul had become Baramullah, and Pulvom, Pulwama. Soldiers deployed almost in every nook and corner of the valley would ensure that the official names were used. Many people had received severe beatings for not obliging. Even the names on hoardings and billboards were regulated during the 1990s.

They finally reached the dervish's abode: he lived in a tidy room of a not-so-tidy house. He was not as old as Salem Apa had made him out to be. It was the flying beard and that imported tasbeeh from Saudi Arabia that made him look ancient.

'The tasbeeh from Saudi is radiant like the moon; its luminescence can lighten up this whole room even in pitch darkness,' the dervish was addressing the gullible audience gathered in the hall.

'The ones your maulvi sahib uses are locally made, they can't even stand the water sprinkles from a week's wadhu (ablution),' he sermonized. 'I have been to Hajj five times. I had the opportunity to take a chopper ride over the holy city. Even the roads over there have noor, a radiance, immersed everywhere you look. That is the place for the pure.'

The audience chanted in response: 'Jazak Allah, Jazak Allah!'

The people assembled there could give competition to the crowd outside Dr Ali's clinic in Sheikh Mohalla. The mud-plastered room was big enough to accommodate over forty people at a time. It was clean, filled with the scent of incense kept on a shelf, next to different translations of the Quran. The floor was covered with a room-sized Kashmiri kaleen. The dervish was sitting in the middle on a raised mattress. The men sat on the right and the women on the left. Bowls filled with dry fruits, a samovar containing kehwa, a kangri from which pungent smoke emanated even during the summer, surrounded the dervish. The house was very cold and calm even at the peak of summer. Since Salem Apa was a regular at the dervish's place, she was allowed to enter the room ahead of many others who had reached before them. They wriggled past a huge crowd of mureeds, the dervish's disciples. Some among the crowd were carrying sweets with them; some carried rice, maize, dry fruits, candies, mutton dishes, cooking oil, and clothes. A couple of people had brought free-sized kameez pyjamas for the dervish. It was as if they had assembled an exhibition.

'What is the need to gift pyjamas to a godman, when most of them don't wear them?' Mubarak asked Salem Apa as they entered the room.

Salem Apa frowned. She hoped the dervish hadn't overheard Mubarak's silly query. But Mubarak was interested in knowing whether the dervish actually wore pyjamas. He was considering verifying by peeping under the godman's soft velvet pheran. He took a place in the men's rows, constantly keeping an eye on Salem Apa and Naziya who were sitting on the other side of the room. The dervish was sitting with his legs folded back, as if he were paralyzed. Bitter, unbreathable smoke came out of the earthen pot he was holding under his ring-laden fingers. The smoke filled every eye in the room with tears.

A woman from the neighbourhood was hurriedly rushed into the room, amidst complaining voices for breaking the code of conduct. The woman's relatives claimed that she had been possessed by a djinn when on her way to collect firewood in a local forest. She needed immediate attention and that was why they had jumped the queue. The dervish directed the woman to be brought to the centre of the room. He ordered her relatives to leave her there and began asking her questions; but the woman wasn't interested in answering them.

'Who are you? Where are you from? What do you want? What would you take to leave?' The dervish's voice was booming in the small room.

When he got absolutely no answers, the dervish slapped the woman and she fainted and fell unconscious. 'She is healed now. I have trapped the djinn in my ring,' he announced, pointing to a stone-ring he was wearing on his little finger. The miracle prompted everyone to chorus again: 'Jazak Allah, Jazak Allah.'

After a while, the dervish whispered in his assistant's ear, who then pointed at Salem Apa. She in turn extended a basket of gifts to him and, as she was about to narrate Mubarak's plight, the godman stopped her.

'He has come for a child. Nothing can remain hidden from the dervish,' he said, to the astonishment of Mubarak and even Salem Apa, whose faith in the dervish reached a new level altogether.

'God tells him everything. He is omnipresent,

omnipotent,' the dervish said, referring to himself in the second person. 'God has given him an extra pair of eyes. Allah has bestowed him with his noor and some of his Ilme-gayab, the knowledge of the unknown.'

He took out a big ripe almond from the pocket of his pheran and began reciting something with his head almost nestling in his stomach. As the peer reached out to Mubarak with his closed fist, an awed Mubarak hesitantly seized his hand and shook it. And then the dervish gave the 'blessed' almond to Naziya, who accepted it with her grateful hands. She held the almond as if it would burn her shivering and frail hands.

Once they were on their way back home, Salem Apa remarked that the couple was indeed very lucky. It was because of her that the peer had listened to them in the very first sitting.

'Buzarg peer does not entertain every one,' she kept boasting until they were back in Shehr-e-Khaas.

After all the bhandaars as ordered by the buzarg peer had been held, a collection of gowns and shoes given to Salem Apa as her fee, and the taweez, amulets, given by the peer—which Mubarak's wife reluctantly soaked in cold thick milk and washed down her gut—something happened. Sana was born. When the nurse at the Lal Ded maternity hospital told him of his daughter's birth, Mubarak hugged Salem Apa, who was by his side through the labour. He then entered the room and picked up Sana, kissed her forehead and announced to his relatives waiting outside: 'My daughter is here.'

While the doctors had not completely ruled out the possibility of Naziya getting pregnant, Mubarak believed that the peer's blessings had helped them. He even went on to promise the dervish a ziyarat, a shrine, on his grave, provided he died before Mubarak. This, of course, had infuriated the peer and Mubarak had to try hard to keep him happy, by sending him various gifts through Salem Apa. Mubarak always reminded her to ask for the peer's pardon: 'Tell the dervish, I never spoke those words! It is my enemies in the neighbourhood who spread the rumours.'

9. A FOR APPLE, T FOR TULIP

THE WINTER WAS receding. A thick white fog, tinged with grey, hung over the city for most of the day. Visibility in the mornings was bad but it would clear up a bit when the dull sun shone in the afternoon for a few hours. And then darkness would descend on the city once again. This year there hadn't been much snowfall—only sporadic rainfall.

In the afternoons, Sana would extend her hand through the metallic window to feel the droplets on her little palm. This opened a new means of connecting with the outside world in this otherwise gloomy time of the year. It convinced her that the world was not coming to an end. A young and gullible Sana had overheard a few elderly women in the neighbourhood talk about a prophecy which suggested that the world was coming to an end. One of the signs of doomsday, according to them, was the days becoming dull, cloudy and extremely cold. It left Sana confused because the young maulvi from Hamza mosque had declared in his powerful voice that on the last day of the universe—the day of qayamat as he referred to it—the sun would be so close to the earth that its heat would melt the mighty mountains, dry up the vast oceans and annihilate even the slightest trace of life on the planet. However, the feel of the raindrops made Sana hopeful about the survival of the world and the coming of spring when she would go to school for the first time.

The snow-clearing machines were rusting in the tents even during the harsh chilai-kalaan. No snowmen flanked the streets this year; only icicles hung from the corners of the roofs.

March had shone brighter, promising a trouble-free summer ahead; children thronged to schools in whites and greys. Markets were upbeat, life full of colours again. The valley bloomed high with expectations, just like the aromatic almond blooms in the surrounding badam vaer (almond garden).

The valley had badly craved some respite from the political uncertainty that had prevailed in the past year.

In the mornings, Sana would sit on the porch of her house. The crows would assemble in the adjacent compound to feed on scattered paddy grains kept on a long mat to dry in the spring sun. Once dry, the paddy would be taken to the nearby mill, where the husk would be separated from the rice. A rat-bed lay beneath the porch, from where the eyes of the rodents gleamed at night like fireflies. Their squeaking could be heard distinctly when they chased each other, and hid from predators.

On a bright Monday, Sana waited for her mother to braid her hair into tiny pleats, which she liked to flaunt over the white of her well-ironed school uniform. Her Funskool shoes, polished black, shone against the sun. They were left against the wall to soften under the spring sun's mild heat. Her feet, which were swollen because of the bone-chilling winter cold and the snow-frost, would take some time to adjust.

'Are they still hurting, jaan?' Sana's mother called out from the balcony as she watched Sana through the translucent glass window.

'Not that much,' Sana mumbled sleepily.

'What? Are they still hurting? I am asking you, Sana! Look up. How are your feet now?' Naziya asked.

The mixture of sunlight and cold winds made Sana too drowsy to pay attention to her mother's repeated queries.

'Jigar, my darling, Ammi is coming in a bit.' Naziya was wearing her usual brown cotton pheran with silver hand-embroidery all over the chest.

'Yes, Ammi, come fast,' Sana said louder this time, as she blocked the sunlight with her hand.

'Yes, my jaan. I'm bringing some cream for your ankles,' said Naziya as she hung trusses of red chillies on the brick wall. It wasn't going to be easy for Sana's feet to adjust to the new school shoes after having worn the red mini duckbacks during chilly winters, Naziya thought.

As Naziya approached the ground floor and sat on the porch next to her daughter, Sana ran her fingers over the tiny crow's feet on the corners of Naziya's eyes. The wrinkles had stories to tell, stories of the taunts and jibes she faced because of her inability to conceive a child early on in her marriage. Things had been difficult for Naziya till Sana arrived in their world. Before that, relatives and friends had even suggested that Mubarak marry a second time.

The Sheikh Manzil had been a difficult new abode for Naziya. However, a lot had changed since Sana was born. Even the house was not the same anymore. When Mubarak's father, Sheikh Rehman, was alive, the balcony used to be an open one. Rehman would sit there on his armchair the whole day smoking his hookah. The space would be flooded with the smoke from the hookah as he kept a watch on his metal shop. It was not too long ago that he had received a state award for his contribution to crafts and metallurgy. Sometimes he would stand and start taking rounds of the balcony, open the window and breathe in the fresh evening air. He would try hard not to nap in the afternoon, but would often fall asleep after lunch. This was when a young Mubarak would surreptitiously inhale tobacco from the hookah. The gurgle as he smoked from the hookah would play in unison with his father's snores.

When Mubarak was young, Rehman never trusted his employees. Rehman would watch the workers the whole time from his balcony—each one of them trembling under his watchful gaze. And when he went down to the drawing room for lunch, he would make Mubarak sit on the armchair and keep an eye on the men in the shop.

One such afternoon when Rehman was in the balcony, Mubarak went to call him for lunch. He got no reply. Rehman lay still in the chair. He was no longer breathing.

~

At Green Fields Play School, a swirl in the dry chinar leaves, which had been swept to a corner of the playground, terrified the children. Sana advanced towards the spot. Unlike other children in the park who held back, she began catching the swirling leaves near the basketball court. 'Look! Satan!' Sana's classmates screamed.

'Where?'

'There it is! Satan!' The children gathered around the swirling leaves. But Sana ignored them all and went chasing after the leaves for a good part of the lunch break. The blood rush had made her face beetroot-red. She was not going to give up that easily.

After a tough chase, Sana was able to grab one of the leaves. She cleaned the leaf on her blue checked skirt. She was quite thrilled with what she had accomplished. She gently placed the leaf on the ground, looked around for the lightest possible stone and placed it over the leaf. Her teacher, who was watching Sana from a distance, had not tried to stop her. While the other children saw Satan swirling in this bunch of leaves, Sana thought she could make some money out of that leaf by keeping it underneath a stone overnight—that is what Sana's mother had told her. She left the leaf there as the lunch break came to an end.

After getting back home in the evening, Sana was eagerly waiting for the next day. Ignoring the homework in front of her, she wondered what she would do with the money she was to collect the next morning. Go on a ride on the ceramic circus horse near the school gate? Or buy an orange candy at the ice-cream stall in the school canteen? Her mind was full of ideas as she chewed on her pencil until her pink tongue turned grey-black.

Next morning at school, Sana looked for her reward under the stone. Unfortunately, she did not find any. *Is my mother a liar?* Sana wondered when she did not get the money she had hoped for. *Or maybe I am the unlucky one. Did I follow the steps properly? Did I tell someone this secret? Did that person come here before me and steal the money? Anyway, I will try again another time*, she thought, while taking small disappointed steps back to her classroom.

A few days later, Sana found a new friend in her school garden: a tulip. It was nine-and-a-half days old, red in colour with a tinge of yellow on its edges. By then she had forgotten about the calf, and the unearned money. But little Sana had no idea that tulips wilt away by the time one realizes they have bloomed—just like the peaceful days in Kashmir. She looked forward to a never-ending friendship, but it was not to be. In a few days she discovered that the scorching sun had had her flower for lunch. There she learned one of life's most difficult lessons: the impermanence of all worldly things.

This was also the time when someone could have told Sana that lightning does not occur when 'a big old dead lady grinds the flour on a mill'. Her mother had often offered that as an explanation to a frightened little Sana. This could also have been the right time to tell her that earthquakes didn't occur due to giant bulls shaking their monstrous heads. Her mother knew Sana would soon seek better answers for these questions. It would no longer be a simple time when 'A' would stand for apple and 'T' for tulip. So, she had requested Mubarak to arrange a suitable tutor for Sana because neither she nor Mubarak thought they were capable of answering her unending volley of questions.

And thus, Samar had agreed to tutor Sana in the evenings when he would usually be free from his studies and after his romantic and idle talks with Rabiya. He was also happy to do it because it would give him frequent access to Mubarak's workshop.

In no time, Samar started looking forward to his evening classes with Sana. After an interesting class during which she learned about robots, Sana had asked Mubarak to make one in his workshop. And without knowing how exactly he'd go about it, Mubarak had started creating one.

10. METAL KINGS

MUBARAK'S METAL WORKSHOP, his family's legacy, continued to bear the brunt of indefinite curfews and strikes. With hardly any orders to fulfil, he had spent the last few months roasting raw chestnuts on a clumsy kerosene stove, waiting for the curfew to be lifted. His workers, some of them daily-wagers, would turn up every morning at Sheikh Manzil in the hope of work. Some of them would come from far-off villages, risking their lives, only to be disappointed at the sight of the closed shutters of the metal shop.

A big hoarding outside the Sheikh Manzil read

'Mubarak Metal Works'. The size of the text on the hoarding was smaller than the name of the painter who had made the sign—Naseem Painters. Many people would come to the shop looking for the painter, and it would send Mubarak into a rage. Sometimes he would shout at them, and sometimes, pretend to be the painter himself and fool them. A few years ago, a gentleman had come in asking for his son's portrait to be painted, and Mubarak agreed to do it. He made the little boy—who had asked his father for a portrait in place of Eidi—sit on a huge carved stone outside the metal shop. He pretended to study the boy's posture and expressions for over half an hour. The boy had patiently obliged and stood still, keeping his head steady in spite of feeling tired. The thought of flaunting the portrait to his friends and schoolmates was incentive enough for him to cooperate with the 'painter'. Mubarak studied him from all angles and in the end he took out a charcoal pen meant to mark his metal designs, and created a sketch of an empty vessel and gave it to the father. The shocked man looked at the disappointed face of his son and started swearing loudly at Mubarak. He even slapped him. An agitated Mubarak and his workers then abused the man using choicest of expletives and asked him to leave: 'Go and tell all those assholes and motherfuckers not to come to my metal shop for portraits and paintings,' Mubarak shouted as the father-son duo left in rage.

During the curfew, Naziya would send endless cups of hot saffron-flavoured kahwa and baekir khaen (a fluffy bread), while Mubarak played carom with his craftsmen outside the metal shop. It was the only way to distract themselves and keep calm while maintaining a watch over the situation. 'Who knows, the curfew may be lifted and we may get some work hours,' Mubarak told his workers as the orders for metal vessels, mostly to be used for marriage ceremonies, piled up and the deadlines kept getting extended.

The saffron turned the kahwa into a delicious yellow-coloured drink. Its delightful heady aroma would stimulate Mubarak's senses. He always imagined that heaven—if at all there was one—would be full of that aroma. This same pleasant smell would travel all the way from his workshop to Samar who lived a few metres away, leaving him craving a sip of that delicious drink.

One Friday afternoon after the prayers, Samar went to visit Mubarak. After a long gap filled with strikes and curfews, the metal workshop was back in business. As Samar approached its entrance, he stood observing the men at work. The sounds of beating of metal grew louder and louder, making it difficult for Mubarak's workers to hear him. Contrary to his image of being a somewhat vague and slightly dull person, Mubarak would become a different person while at work in the metal shop. He would instruct his craftsmen to make the most of the normal days—like a commander marshalling his troops for a secret mission.

When Samar came to the shop, Mubarak, in a brown pheran with chestnuts in hand, was shouting instructions at his craftsmen rapidly. Right next to the door was the municipality roller, which most women in the area used as a clothes-stand. Some children would play football, using its giant metal tyres as a goalpost; and some others used it as wickets while playing cricket. Samar approached Mubarak who was standing amidst the metal dust. The nearby furnace radiated translucent red heat, which warmed the whole workshop. The workers and everything in the shop acquired a hot-red hue under the light emanating from the furnace. The radiance had a divine quality to it and it immediately lifted Samar's mood. Mubarak greeted Samar, and they chitchatted about Mubarak's workshop and Samar's studies. Soon they were enjoying the kahwa in vintage bone china cups that Naziya sent downstairs. Mubarak looked around his workshop with the gaze of a proud owner.

'Do you know what metal work is all about?' he asked Samar.

Samar chose not to answer that question. He was more interested in the cup of saffron kahwa in front of him. Its aroma had often drawn Samar to Mubarak's workshop. But upon reaching, he would be disappointed to see empty cups, left in a corner after the workers had relished the drink. However, this time Samar was lucky.

And then after finishing the last drop of his

kahwa as Mubarak droned on about metal work, Samar finally mustered the courage to tell Mubarak why he was there. He wanted to talk to Mubarak about his relationship with Rabiya and get him on his side. There was no one other than Mubarak whom Samar could trust with this information.

'I suspected that you were interested in that girl when I saw you staring at her in the matador all those months ago. I was worried about Sana's education and there you were, staring that girl,' Mubarak said, smiling. 'Let me see what I can do about it.'

But not much could be done as another period of strikes and curfew began. The workshop had its shutters down and looked like an abandoned mill. The only person who was happy about the curfew was Shakeel Mirza. The strikes worked in his favour, as he used them as an excuse for reaching office late. He would even skip office work sometimes in order to finish other commitments at home.

Once when Mirza and Mubarak got into an argument over the noise coming from the workshop, Mirza had announced in rage, 'I will complain to the authorities. How can this land grabber carry on like this in a residential area?'

Mirza had grown weary of the racket the workshop caused. Although the workshop had always been there, the racket had increased, especially after Mubarak expanded his workshop by encroaching on the land that was a part of the road in front of it. He had managed to do so by bribing some officials, and in turn had made enemies in the neighbourhood. He would often end up fighting with people who reminded him of this.

After all those trips to Mubarak's workshop, Samar knew that no matter how much people, including his father, hated Mubarak, the man was a master in metalwork. Samar never let his father's tiff with Mubarak come in the way of his friendship with him, and the later reciprocated in equal measure. Mubarak and his employees could construct practically anything from metal: from their world famous cutlery sets to locally marketed household tools. The bronze and copper utensils displayed on the emerald-green shelves of his shop would hypnotize his customers. And the customized gold- and silver-bottomed vessels were one of a kind. His intricately designed vessels were a symbol of prestige in most homes. And although Shakeel did not like the sound of hammering and drilling coming from the workshop, deep down, he too acknowledged Mubarak's artistry. He often admired Mubarak's delicate touches and his painstaking refinement. He even bought a set of silver plates from him. These plates had deep, flat beds and 'Mubarak Metalworks' engraved on the bottom of each in copper. Samar tried to feel 'the prestige' in those heavy plates but all he felt was a faint silvery smell. Finally, he settled for the lighter bone china plates, which he could carry onto the portico and enjoy his food while basking in the sunshine. Those princely metal plates made his wrists ache.

Samar often ended up hanging out in the university corridors, using the ongoing political unrest and clashes as an excuse to skip classes. He would hang out with friends who lived in the university hostel. There were no cinema halls in the valley so going to the movies for entertainment was out of question.

Samar and Rabiya had progressed from holding hands in the matador to kissing more often in the botanical garden, deserted parks and sometimes in Samar's father's car. The question of anything more didn't even arise in this conservative and deeply religious society. Although many of his friends and even Rauf goor claimed that they had slept with many women whom they wouldn't name, Samar never believed them. He assumed they were all made up stories meant to entertain but not to be taken seriously.

Samar's father neither meddled in his affairs, nor gave him religious sermons to be an obedient son like many other parents did. But Samar still sought his approval and wanted to live the life that was expected of him.

11. ANOTHER DAY IN PARADISE

Every place of this land is beautiful; every mountain
is a darling,
Sky is the abode of this land; its blue is immersed in
the waters of Dal!

A MONTH LATER, things started settling down in the valley. There was an influx of tourists with the advent of spring. Some attributed the pleasure of having an early spring to global warming. Several countries had lifted travel advisories issued to their citizens, cautioning them of the perceived danger associated with their travel to the valley. This step had been taken after the successful winter games held in January at the popular skiing resort of Gulmarg.

People were coming to the valley from all over the world. Some first timers praised the beauty of the valley while others who had visited Kashmir before, during the romantic '70s and '80s, were disappointed. They had seen the past: when the Dal's water was scintillating and clear; when doonga boats plied in the mesmerizing waters of the Jhelum, which acted as the great artery of the valley; and when waazwan, the traditional thirty-six-course feast of Kashmir, was served in its true glory. The valley lived up to the challenge it had thrown to the world ever since the famous poet Amir Khusrau purportedly described it in Persian as 'Heaven on Earth':

Gar Firdous baroye zameen ast,
Hamin asto, hamin asto, hamin ast
(If there is a heaven on earth,
It's here, it's here, it's here)

It is said that when the mighty Mughal king Jehangir was asked on his deathbed about his cherished desire, he said: 'Kashmir, the rest is worthless.'

The rides in the waters of Kashmir in the moonlight were a wonder of the past now. Conflict and corruption had turned its once rejuvenating sweet waters turgid and stale. That aura could now only be recalled but certainly not re-created. The warmth of yore floated in the hazy skies now.

It was during this gloomy but nonetheless welcome tourist season that Rosaline, a New York-based woman, made her first visit to Kashmir. She was travelling alone as her husband Douglas, a Wall Street banker, had cancelled his ticket at the last minute because of a work commitment that required him to stay back. With the tickets booked and all the arrangements for their stay in New Delhi and Srinagar made, Rosaline decided to travel solo on this trip of a lifetime. Moreover, this tour had come at the right time for Rosaline. Her relationship with Douglas was going through a rough patch. His unending work engagements had been increasing of late and she was fed up with them. His assignments would keep him busy, and he would constantly travel across the length and breadth of the US. And even when he was at home, he would be on call with his bosses and clients or be online replying to and sending emails. He would coordinate with clients across time zones. She felt lonely at times and occasionally rued marrying the busy Wall Street banker.

What Rosaline saw as her plane approached the cliffs of the Pir Panjaal Mountains in the valley was nothing less than a portrait drawn on a canvas by a master artist. To her, Van Gogh's magic faded in front of the ultra-white knife strokes on the steep brown and blue mountains and the revitalizing greens of apple and walnut orchards. Green rice fields that would later turn golden seemed like a patchwork quilt.

As she reached the airport's foreign tourist registration section, just outside the arrival gates, she clutched her red bag tightly. It contained all her cash, cards and documents, including her passport. A young man spotted her at the reception and guided her towards a swarm of white government taxis. The taxi drivers beckoned her, each offering a lesser amount to drive her to her destination. She boarded the one that looked comparatively cleaner than the rest, and they sped off, amidst jealous glances from other taxi drivers. The foreigners always paid more—everyone knew that. Looking out from her window, Rosaline was surprised by the presence of huge contingents of armed forces. She saw the men in khaki patrolling the roads in bullet-proof trucks, manning the gates of hospitals and schools, and various checkposts. Shabby bunkers made of cement bags piled up on one another and manned with armed men and enclosed in razor wire encroached the buildings and roads in almost all corners of the city.

'What is all this army doing here?' Rosaline asked the driver. Last time she had heard the news, India and Pakistan were not at war. Had it broken out while she was on her way from America? She shifted uncomfortably in her seat. Why would her husband not travel with her at a time like this?

In one look from the rear-view mirror, the driver took in her expensive-looking clothes that reflected her expensive upbringing. *Of course she would ask such a question*, he thought, giving her a smug look in the mirror. *The worst hardship she must have faced in her well-protected country was probably when her kid got admission to the second-best school in the neighbourhood.*

'In your country the army comes like locusts in the season of war, and then returns for good. But in mine they'll stay till every last one of us...' He left the sentence hanging in mid-air.

Rosaline knew she wouldn't be able to extract more out of him. She cursed the travel books she had read to get all possible information on Kashmir. They all talked about the beautiful hills, Dal Lake and shikara rides but not one had mentioned this ever-present barrage of army men. Everything here—the buildings, the shops, the roads, expressions on people's faces and even the stray animals—suggested something was wrong.

She vaguely remembered a book that mentioned the Kashmir of the '70s. She made a mental note to check the publication dates once she got back, and to give Douglas a scolding for being careless. She was strangely missing his presence. He would have calmed her nerves, told her that the army uniform was probably the latest fashion trend in the valley or something equally frivolous. Together, they would have laughed it off.

She changed the topic and had some unrelated conversation with the driver until she reached Hotel Mount Kashmir, overlooking the Dal. It was situated on a mountain carved out of the Sulaiman Hill. Rosaline noticed that there was a market nearby. Perhaps she could buy authentic pashmina shawls, wooden souvenirs like shikara replicas and papier maché boxes of different shapes, she thought.

On her fifth day in the valley, Rosaline was walking with her guide in the historic downtown. She happened to pass by Mubarak's metal shop and a beautiful cutlery set on display caught her attention. She entered the shop replete with metal vessels. Mubarak was sitting in a corner, inhaling his hookah. On seeing Rosaline, his assistant Haleem directed Mubarak's attention towards her. Rosaline shuffled through the shop, browsing through the various vessels and artifacts on display and finally settled for the cutlery set that she had initially seen. She requested her guide to find out the price.

By now Mubarak had set his hookah aside and was ready to attend to his firang customer. While Rosaline was busy appreciating the metal works, Mubarak had been watching her. She was dressed rather attractively in a white blouse and a blue denim skirt. He couldn't help but notice her peachy-white legs. The guide asked him for the price, but instead of replying to the guide, Mubarak picked up the cutlery set and approached Rosaline directly.

'Look at this set, madam. It is the best you will get in Kashmir,' he managed to say in whatever little English he knew. Rosaline's guide got his guard up and felt like he would soon be jobless if all metal-shop owners learnt to speak the firang zubaan. The guide interrupted him and again asked for the price of the cutlery set.

'Three thousand two hundred,' Mubarak casually replied.

'He is quoting a much higher price than it actually merits,' the guide whispered in Rosaline's ear. 'Let's look elsewhere. We will find it at a cheaper price,' he said, trying to lead Rosaline away from Mubarak's flirtatious gaze.

As Rosaline was about to leave, she asked Mubarak directly for a discount. It had been a lean day for Mubarak, so he thought for a while and then agreed to reduce the price.

'Two thousand and eight hundred rupees. Final price!' he told Rosaline directly, with the guide feeling a bit left out.

'He's still charging a higher price, madam. I am telling you, let's check out some other place. There are so many of them,' he held Rosaline's arm and started walking out of the shop, when Mubarak stopped them, confronting the guide and accusing him of earning commission from other shopkeepers.

Rosaline stopped for a moment and was convinced that it was a good bargain. She suspected that her looks had earned her a decent discount but didn't care much about it. She liked the cutlery set so much that she would have paid the original price for it, had Mubarak not agreed to reduce it.

Mubarak asked Haleem to pack the set in an exquisitely carved walnut wooden box. In the meanwhile, Mubarak tried drawing Rosaline's attention to the other items in his workshop, especially the samovar he had been working on. Rosaline politely refused and thanked him for the box and left.

Rosaline had given the other items on display another look from the corner of her eye as she was leaving the metal shop. The beautiful designs and delicate handwork were tempting, but she told Mubarak she would come another time for them. This raised Mubarak's hopes and he promised her a good discount on her next visit.

'Do tourists necessarily have to deal through guides?' Mubarak was disappointed at not getting the opportunity to talk at length to the foreign 'mem'. He watched Rosaline walk away, while he settled on his seat and started putting coal in the bowl of the hookah to prepare the chilum. As Rosaline disappeared from view, he added a fistful of hard tobacco on the hot coal. Taking deep gushes from the hookah, he pictured Rosaline as she first stepped into the shop; thc image hit him and transported him to another world.

During her stay in Srinagar, Rosaline explored the tourist sites of the valley. She visited its lush gardens reminiscent of the mighty Mughals, and paid her respects at the sacred shrines of revered Sufi saints. She even conquered many mighty peaks as she made the mandatory visits to Gulmarg in the north and Pahalgam in the south.

Mubarak kept a close watch every day at the entrance of his metal shop, looking for Rosaline. Thinking about Rosaline all the time, anticipating her visit had made him restless. In the afternoons, he would venture out on a stroll all along the street, right up to the main Chowk.

'She could be looking for our shop. She can easily lose sight of it amidst the trail of shops and wander around,' he told Haleem. Mubarak's endless detours of the street made his wife and other workers suspicious. They started talking behind his back and even tried getting more information from Haleem about their master's behaviour. They, however, could not extract much out of him.

'Mubarak sahib is a busy man. He has many

things on his mind. He takes a walk around in the afternoon to de-stress and think about how to expand his business,' he would often quip, shrugging them all away.

One afternoon, Mubarak followed a lady wearing faded denims and a crop top for a long time. He walked behind her at a brisk pace, trying to catch up with her. As he reached closer to the woman, he called for her in his broken English, 'Miss, Mubarak, Miss'.

To his surprise, it was some other tourist and she hurled abuses at Mubarak. Onlookers also stared at him and ridiculed him till he explained his position to them. Because most people in the area knew him, Mubarak was let off.

12. THE WAITING

SAMAR HAPPENED TO be home one day as he didn't have to attend classes. He was taking a nap in the drawing room and got some shut eye for a brief moment, only to be disturbed by a dream in which Rabiya had smiled at him in the same way she smiled when she would walk past him with her friends in the university campus.

The weather department had predicted rains for the next four days, and that the heatwave across the state would start easing from the next day onwards. This prediction had come over a week ago and there had been no sign of rain so far in Kashmir's cerulean blue skies.

The weather in Kashmir had changed over the years, and the four seasons were only a part of school textbooks. There were only two seasons now: nail-biting cold and scorching heat. Why don't they change the textbooks, Samar wondered, thinking of Sana's books which mentioned the four seasons as mausame-bahaar, mausame-garma, mausame-khizaan and mausame-sarma (spring, summer, autumn and winter).

As Samar made lemon and mint sherbat for everyone, his father returned from the zuhr prayer, which he occasionally attended on his days off from work. He would go to the nearby Jamiah masjid. This mosque was one of the oldest and had papier-maché mehraabs and motifs of birds and trees on its walls. A hoarding outside the masjid read: Kya aapko nimaz ke liye fursat nahi, Tajub hai! (It is an irony that you don't find time for prayers.)

When Samar handed over a glass of the sherbet to his father, Mirza seemed disturbed.

'What happened, Baba?' Samar asked his father.

'Where should I begin?' Mirza said, sounding

frustrated. Then continued, 'Some young men had assembled outside the mosque. They must have been around seventeen to twenty years old, and were discussing the upcoming cricket match between their club and another team. Just then the imam asked them to join him for Allah ka zikr, the Almighty's mention. Now, this imam is around the same age as the boys and used to be a wicketkeeper in their team. He had even won the man of the match award for his team in a local cricket tournament once. Just a few months ago, he was one of them it seems. He used to dress like the other youngsters in the group. He wore denims, wristbands, shaved his facial hair and spoke about movies and girls. But he had suddenly gone outside the state to train as an imam. He now wears a long white gown and sports a flowing beard, applies ittar on his neck and soorma in his eyes.

'He started his talk by addressing everyone. The boys in the audience instantly broke into a roar of laughter; they found it hard to control themselves even though the talk was about Allah. This, of course annoyed the imam, „Astaghfuruallah.

God forbid. You shouldn't be laughing when the topic is such that even the angels are paying close attention„ he said unperturbed, and continued sermonizing.« It is important to be a good doctor, an engineer, a sportsperson, a teacher. But, what is paramount is that we should be good Muslims first.„ He was saying that our aamal (deeds) should be righteous and our character should be like that of the Prophet. May Allah's peace and Mercy be upon him.

'I was absolutely absorbed in the discourse. But when the imam left, those young men started talking about him. They didn't think he was religious at all or fit for the role of a maulvi. They were saying things like:« How can this drifter fill the shoes of the Prophet? How can he be in the space that the Prophet once occupied? Until yesterday he wore a Nike cap and branded trousers. What example will he set for society?„'

Shakeel Mirza couldn't comprehend why the boys were talking so dismissively about the imam. 'What does wearing Nike caps have to do with religious values? How is it sacrilegious?' He asked

Samar. 'These hypocrites couldn't say it to the imam's face. If they had the guts, they should have brought this up with him rather than talking behind his back,' he said as Samar lifted his head in attention. Samar had no answer to his father's questions.

As Kashmiri Sufi music played in the background, Samar tried to change his father's mood by singing along with the magical voice of Rashid Hafiz: 'Chouri cholhum yawan chooro lo lo, kyaze logthas aeshqeni tandoori lo lo...' He wasn't sure what else could help.

But Mirza continued his rant, 'These misguided youth have ample time and nothing to do with it. So they take refuge in religion. Everybody takes religion, breaks it and manipulates it to justify their own purpose. They fail to understand that nobody has a monopoly over morality.'

'Yes,' Samar nodded in agreement. And then they discussed the politicization of religious places, how some groups in the mosque fought over petty issues like whether it should have a loudspeaker or not.

'May God bestow some wisdom on them and remove all the possible hurdles in society which could come in the way of my union with Rabiya,' Samar prayed as he looked outside his window at the faint outline of the Persian-style dome of the Jamiah Mosque. As Samar had recently discovered from Mubarak's enquiries, Rabiya's father, Akbar Hilal, swore by the Mirwaiz of Kashmir and his family. He was an avowed Bakra. He believed in the evils of the Sheikh like he would believe in the Holy Book. There were no second thoughts: it was only the Mirwaiz who had a vision for the future of Kashmir. He even opposed the views of another hardliner separatist, calling his dealings redundant and obsolete.

13. THE LAST RIDE

SALEM APA AGREED, on Mubarak's insistence, to talk to Shakeel Mirza about Samar's relationship with Rabiya and his wish to marry her. Although Samar's parents didn't have any problems with the idea, they were adamant that Samar first complete his LLM and then start practicing at court.

'He is still young, he must complete his studies and start earning. Marriage can wait,' said Shakeel Mirza. 'After all what good is a man who can't even bring bread home. They can get engaged in the meanwhile,' he said.

'And we can do a background check on the family,' Samar's mother said out of concern.

'I am sure Samar has factored in the caste, family background and other things,' Salem Apa assured her.

Samar was ecstatic. It would be foolish not to send the marriage proposal to Rabiya's family, Mubarak told him.

~

In another corner of Srinagar, near Dal Lake, it seemed to Rosaline that she would never forget the sight of the lake at sunset, when the colours of the pigeons changed from white to grey, then grey to black in the dusk. It was a miracle of nature she had never paid heed to before. The skyline was almost invisible in a blur of pastel grey, and the mountains were glowing on the top. The shade of the sky reflected a wisp of grey smoke, with the horizon of the setting sun emerging radiant with pink light. Rosaline had never witnessed anything like this before.

Sitting in the shikara, Rosaline realized that she had actually lived each moment instead of mindlessly going about her days. It was ironic though: how was she finding comfort in the chaos of a place riddled with conflict and among people marginalized and trampled upon for centuries? But the trip had taught her an unexpected lesson: to not take the small blessings in her life for granted. But her biggest learning was the importance of spending time with one's family, something which Douglas seldom did after their marriage. The solitude had taught her things she had never given a thought to before.

She gazed at the chinar trees in front of her. Beneath their shade, young men were playing carom, sitting on some stones picked up from a nearby construction site. The arrangement was such that only four boys could play at a time while many others waited patiently for their turn before dusk could set in. Thus, only a few lucky ones would get to play this evening while the rest would have to be content watching. But nobody complained. After the dark night and the succeeding day, they would all gather again and continue the game.

Rosaline was deep in thought throughout the

shikara ride. The churning waters compounded the chaos in her mind. The memories of her husband had become inconsequential now. The strokes of the wooden oar cutting through water were hypnotic. She tried hard to see her reflection in the water, but it was blurred. As the heart-shaped oar in the hands of the shikarawala's hands swirled her image in the water, she wished to merge her past and her present.

The view from the waters of Dal was breathtaking. There were lush mountains on one side where Rosaline could see guest houses, official residences, the carved Pari Mahal, the Shankaracharya temple on the way, Taj Vivanta Hotel and the grand Mughal Gardens. The other side of the view included the Hari Parbat, the Makhdoom Sahib and Hazratbal Shrine. The view would be clear till just before autumn. Later the chinars would take a different form: naked, bare! Interwoven branches like steel wool would be on display all winter until spring returned and infused life into them. Thinking about the possibilities this quaint town offered, Rosaline wished she could spend her whole life in that yellow shikara and swim over the pristine expanse of the lake—but she had to return to America, that's where she belonged.

Suddenly her reverie was broken by the sight of the mighty Zabarwan that the shikarawala pointed out to her. Rosaline remembered reading about the mountains that looked like twins hugging each other. But what she was seeing now was a stark contrast. While the hill on the right bore tall, proud trees, the other was naked, bereft of its green crown. She could make out faint outlines of some ongoing construction work on the left one. 'You people are lucky to stay in this beautiful place. But you don't care for it. How can you let something which nourishes, protects and feeds you die?' she asked the boatman, frustrated by the ugly sight of the construction and the algal blooms eating into the lake from all sides.

The soiled face of the boatman broke into a smile which produced tiny crinkles at the corner of his eyes, 'Miss Roa-zhy-lheen,' he began in his broken English. He had realized early on in his career that he would be able to attract more customers if he could talk to those 'boot-suit people' in their language. 'See those encroachments? They come up every day. They get dismantled every day. But they refuse to die,' he said, pointing towards some makeshift tin sheds haphazardly thrown together. They had come up that very morning after officials from the Lakes and Waterways Development Authority (LAWDA) had destroyed them the previous night as usual. A group of people had surrounded the area and were raising slogans: 'LAWDA Murdabad. Down with LAWDA! LAWDA hai hai, gali gali mein shor hai LAWDA chor hai...' The boatman raised his voice so as to be audible and asked, 'Tell me, Miss, if they are illegal, how do they get electricity? Who gives them ration cards?' Rosaline was silent.

Amidst the slogans and chants of the people, they drew near the char-chinari, a small landmass at the centre of Dal, named after the four chinar trees that adorned it. 'Those trees, Miss, have been there for hundreds of years. Badshah Akbar planted them,' he informed her, as the chants and slogans began to fade.

Rosaline looked at the golden-brown carpet of fallen chinar leaves. They would easily be crushed by the touch of a finger and disappear into thin air. In a rather dramatic moment, she wished she could blow with the breeze like the chinar leaves.

Like all shikarawalas, this man too preferred not to ply during the night as it could take a toll on the eyesight, and so Rosaline had to return to life on land. It was, as usual, windy and chilly at night around Dal. She walked on a dark street leading towards her hotel room. Wolves had started howling in the dark somewhere, announcing the night. Life in the city came to a standstill after eight in the evening: shops would shut down; offices would close; hawkers would go home; and birds would return to their nests. Only rodents, journalists and dogs would remain in the streets. And also troops of armed men who seemed ghostly in the calm and cold of the night.

Rosaline noticed that there were many houseboats on the Dal with foreign names. There was one named 'Shielaan'—apparently a British tourist had named it after his two daughters Shiela and Ann. There was another one called 'Helen of Troy'. And there were others named 'Joan of Arc' and 'Alexandra'. There was one named after her homeland too: 'Houseboat New York'.

Amidst the high-pitched noise of crickets and other nocturnal insects, Rosaline reached her hotel room. She wondered why she hadn't visited the valley until now. She promised herself she wouldn't stay stationed in her comfortable and cosy apartment in New York. She would travel the world and discover herself in new places.

As she walked into her room, she looked across the window facing the Dal. Groups of men and women were singing a melancholic song, bringing an end to another hard day. The women had made their children sit under kerosene lanterns hanging from the deodar wood of the houseboats. Some fisherwomen, who had been busy selling fresh black trout in the day, were washing their vessels and readying them for the next morning. Men with hard, grimy faces were counting their day's income.

The boatmen had seen it all by now. They

knew how hard it would be for their children to survive if they were not well educated. Even the exquisite houseboats didn't bring much income anymore. Moreover, the number of houseboats had dwindled with time, as had the number of tourists in the strife-torn valley. Not many people even knew how to construct houseboats anymore. The future looked bleak. Tourism was running dry, and people had small savings to live through the off-season. Those associated with the trade had started looking for other means of livelihood. Amidst the strikes and curfews, they wanted a better future for their children, one which would allow them to live a respectable life.

~

One afternoon, Rosaline visited Mubarak's shop. This was the fifth time in eight days. And this time it was without a guide, which added to Mubarak's joy. But Rosaline's frequent visits to the metal shop were beginning to bother Naziya. On the one hand Rosaline brought business; and on the other, it was increasing Mubarak's obsession with Rosaline.

Naziya had overheard Haleem tell his co-workers that Rosaline had once complimented Mubarak's 'Greek God' looks. Mubarak's behaviour over the last few days had also been different than usual. He was spending more time in the bath, applying ittar all over his body, trimming his stubble and wearing freshly ironed western clothes every day. He was avoiding his usual khan suits. He had even placed orders for two pleated suits at Subhaan Tailors, which was one of the best in the city. He applied soorma to highlight his emerald-green eyes, which stood out distinctly on his face and against his long, black wavy hair. Naziya noticed that he had been applying Rogan Badaam Shereen oil—the expensive almond oil—on his already-toned body. Mubarak's handsomeness exemplified the proud ancestry of Kashmiris as the descendants of Alexander of Macedonia's army.

Mubarak had never been conscious of his looks; never had he explored himself like this for hours together. And his wife had never been as anxious about her husband's looks, as she had been after discovering them through the eyes of another woman. The other woman—even the thought made Naziya nervous. She was convinced that her husband was falling in love with Rosaline.

One evening, Naziya decided to carry kahwa herself to her husband's shop rather than have one of the craftsmen collect it. These days she felt the need to be close to her husband as much as possible. She would hover over Mubarak with a grim determination, as if to signal to the white woman that he 'belonged' to her. As she was pouring kahwa from the samovar, Rosaline appeared at the workshop to say a final goodbye to Mubarak and his team of wonderful craftsmen. Rosaline asked Mubarak if he could give her a little tour of the workshop so that she could document his metal work for an article that she intended to write after returning. Mubarak took this opportunity and signalled Haleem and the other workers to leave. As Rosaline walked ahead of him, expressing her admiration for the workshop, Mubarak wanted to ask her about her family, her job, her likes and dislikes. But his limited knowledge of the English language was an impediment he couldn't do much about at that moment. So instead he just followed Rosaline as she clicked photos of the place. When she showed him the photos later, all he could say was, 'Masha Allah, Masha Allah!' Rosaline smiled every time Mubarak uttered those godly words. As their little tour came to an end and Rosaline spoke her final words to Mubarak and his workers, Naziya's eyes darted from Rosaline's expressionless face to Mubarak's crestfallen one.

14. THE FORBIDDEN MAHAL

ON A SUNNY day in Shehr-e-Khaas—a name which many inhabitants of the area insisted should be used instead of 'downtown'—Sana was restless. She was going on her first school picnic, and it would also be the first time that she would be spending time with her friends outside the classroom. The sun was shining brightly after a long spell of rains. She had had a bath the previous evening because the children were supposed to reach the school by seven in the morning. Naziya was worried Sana might catch a cold if she bathed in the early hours.

Sana had prepared a list of items with her

friend Pintoji for this special occasion. Mubarak had happily bought everything on her little list. Sana excitedly took the bag full of goodies from Mubarak. Her green eyes had gleamed last night as she removed a guava-juice box, the chocolates and the potato chips, and the colourful hairpin that Mubarak had added as a surprise.

But today, Sana was not happy with Pintoji. When he saw Sana at the gate of Sheikh Manzil, dressed in her crisp, freshly ironed uniform he came running to her.

'Do you remember Tufail, the long-haired guy who owns the bookshop near Nowhatta?'

Sana had faint memories of Tufail. He always gave her free éclairs whenever Mubarak took her to his store to buy crayons or chalks—but she didn't have the time for this. This Pinto-Binto was always doing this, she thought, always taking her mind off more important things at hand.

'They got him. Those green men. My daddy said he was simply at the wrong place at the wrong time. He got caught while playing the stone-throwing game. Daddy said it is forbidden.'

Sana was disturbed. Another one? Why do grown-ups play this game when it hurts? Why can't they play something else? Cricket maybe? She wondered whether the Barbarshah road would be closed today because of this. Sana was worried that they would have to take the longer route if the road was closed and that would delay the picnic. She looked sadly at her bag; the chocolates had already started melting. There were five: three milk chocolates and two dark brown nutty ones. The brown ones would make her teeth look ugly, she thought and decided to give them to her friends. Maybe she should give one to Pinto—he was always displaying his shiny whites. But what if the school bus never came to pick her up? Pintoji's eyes were peeled on the road waiting for a peek of that yellow bus. As every minute ticked by, Pintoji kept giving her his I-told-you-so look. Suddenly, a familiar honking at the corner brought sunshine on Sana's face. There it was, a yellow bus, tiny hands waving at her from its windows. A banner hung on its sides, 'GREEN FIELDS ON EXCURSION.' Sana looked at Pinto smugly, and stuck out her tongue at him and got into the bus.

On the way, the children were singing a song when their teacher interrupted, 'First a recitation to ensure a safe picnic,' she said. Everybody grudgingly hurried through it. And then they continued singing popular Bollywood songs.

Amidst all the wonderful chaos, Sana's teacher couldn't help but think about Tufail. She regularly visited his shop to buy stationary for the school. Looking at those innocent children, she wondered why people grow up at all. As children, they are naïve and innocent and don't care about or understand the political situation. But unlike children from the other parts of the country, the children of Kashmir can't escape the curfews, killings and conflict around them. When do these children realize that they are living in a conflict zone where larger games are at play? Does it take away the innocence of the games they play on the field? She remembered the first time she was caught in a cross fire and pellet shelling. It had changed her world. That game was nothing like the games she had played. There was blood all around, people who died never woke up, unlike in her games at school. The cries of people were real rather than made up. The pain was real.

As the bus stopped at a checkpost a few metres away from the Dal Lake, the children realized they had embarked on the way to Pari Mahal. The Mahal, built by the Mughal prince Dara Shikoh, was situated on a cliff in the Zabarwan hills, and the road climbed through a dense forest-like enclave with the Governor's House, the Shankaracharya temple and many other guest houses on the way. The shade of the trees created an illusion of night. Sana peeped through the window of the bus. She saw a colourful creature with turquoise, cerulean and orange tints. It was the only visible thing among the dark green pedestals of the forest. She asked her teacher what it was. Must be a colourful kingfisher carrying a ripe fry fish in its mouth, came the reply. The fish was twitching inside the long beak of the kingfisher while its tail was wagging in the air. The bird escorted the bus all the way to the Mahal and then disappeared. The Mahal was at a frog's eye view from the Dal as it gazed on its naked waters from the hillock. Sana visualized the

Pari Mahal of her bedtime stories as a place full of white fairies. She imagined the place was a dream abode with many milk ponds, never-dying tulips and fairies playing hide and seek with white rabbits with pink bums. What magic did the fairies use to help those hairy creatures dig tunnels beneath the orange-green carrot beds in and around the Mahal? But when the bus stopped near the entrance, the place was different from what she had imagined. It was only the ruins of an observatory, half buried in the mountain as if the king who built it had sucked its expanse when he had died. Its turrets were manned by machine guns and barracks. But its cavernous echoing corridors carried a heady sense of romance.

The Mahal she saw was carved out of the mountain, resembling the Hanging Gardens of Babylon she had heard about. She saw bunkers with armed men guarding the rectangular nooks of its several step gardens. Crows and pigeons were skirting around, playing with nuts. Some trees provided them with a hunting ground on their long canopies, which reached sky high. On this high ground, which was almost above the clouds, it drizzles beneath your feet.

An afternoon game with friends landed Sana in the backyard of the Mahal, where she saw an old chinar tree with an exposed funnel-shaped black trunk. Its branches missing, its slithery bark was like that of an eel on which birds, irrespective of their size and stature, struggled to land. The bedtime stories never mentioned this tree. Sana went near it, touched its hollow surface on which names and signs scribbled by lovers withered its hard wood. There was a secret door inside the tree that led to the dense bushes behind. To the kingdom of genies and fairies, Sana thought. What treasure awaited her behind that door?

She advanced towards the bushes and saw empty biscuit and potato chips wrappers and cold-drink bottles scattered around. So this is what the genies have for breakfast, she decided.

She called out for her friends to help her unravel the secrets behind the dark door. As nobody turned up, Sana went ahead nervously and pushed the mat that separated the human world from her fairytale. What she saw inside was a couple, behind the parapet of green grass, embracing each other like two snakes entwined firmly. They were startled by the noise of her little feet. Sana's voice made them draw away from each other. To her astonishment, it was Samar, and with him was Rabiya. Sana approached the couple and broke into a giggle which was followed by a big chuckle and later a laugh, in which both Samar and Rabiya joined her. Before Sana dropped out of nowhere, Samar had been consoling Rabiya. Her father had warned her against meeting Samar. He had learned of their relationship from Rabiya's mother after Rabiya had finally opened up to her about her intention to marry Samar.

Samar gestured at Sana to keep quiet and accompanied her to the garden where other students were taking joyrides on a mobile swing. Just then their teacher started head counts and the picnic came to an end.

The next day when Sana turned up for her tuition, Samar begged her not to disclose anything of what she had seen the other day. Sana agreed to keep his little secret, provided Samar agreed to get her chocolates and a horse-on-wheels.

As Sana started reciting a poem, Samar's thoughts strayed back to Pari Mahal. He was worried about Rabiya. He couldn't imagine his life without her and was thinking of ways to win over her father.

And then suddenly Sana interrupted his thoughts by talking about Pari Mahal, which also drew the attention of her parents. When Samar was in school, the Pari Mahal was forbidden to the public. Locals were not allowed to visit the fort. Only people with VIP passes and considerable clout could go there. Through Sana's eyes, Naziya and Mubarak got a glimpse of the place for the first time. She described how Srinagar could be seen from up there. How the houses looked like matchboxes and vehicles like ants. And of course, the legendary tulip garden on the foothills of Zabarwan.

When Pintoji wasn't willing to interact with the world, his self-imposed house arrest made him explore new dimensions of life at home. One of his favourite things to do was to form friendships with his possessions—like the black-and-white TV set in his father's room or the soldier clock which would wake him up on lonely mornings.

One day when he was in the washroom, he felt a little suffocated and dizzy. He opened the window with some effort. Just then a dreadful-looking creature crept inside. It was hanging on to the outer walls of the bathroom, making a feast of the houseflies and mosquitoes. Pintoji was sure it would try to enter the bathroom through the window later at night. Disgust filled him and he tried to squash it under his feet, but the creature was too fast for him. He damaged the edge of the cemented wall as the creature disappeared.

The next day when Pinto was on the toilet seat, he saw some movement on the floor. As Pinto lowered his head, he saw a tiny parachute-like thing gliding from a silky thread in the same way as Spiderman. As the spider landed on the white tiles, it extended its joints and its long legs became visible and distinct from its small body. Pintoji turned on the nearby tap. Water dripped on the floor and the creature retreated into the thin thread. This fascinated Pintoji.

15. PINTO AND THE WITNESS CLOCK

ONE AFTERNOON IN July, violent clashes between the youth and the soldiers broke out near the Ghanta Ghar located in the city centre, Lal Chowk. The protest had broken after a moderate religious preacher had been shot point blank outside the nearby masjid, while he was cycling towards the grand mosque for evening prayers. As the news spread, many young men pelted stones at policemen, who responded with tear gas shells, rubber bullets and pellet guns, injuring scores of them.

Mubarak, who was returning from his brother-in-law's house in uptown Srinagar, was hit in the head by a stone. Luckily for Mubarak, Pintoji happened to be passing by in an auto. He spotted an injured Mubarak and with the driver's help carried him into the auto, and they at once set out for the nearby clinic. Mubarak's wounds were dressed up and Pintoji then dropped him home in the same auto.

Pintoji had come to Lal Chowk to collect his bicycle from a mechanic when he stumbled upon the injured Mubarak lying on the street. Pintoji had developed a certain immunity against tear gas shells. His senses had stopped reacting to their bitter, pungent smell.

The clock at the Ghanta Ghar, the Marxist-inspired red tower, was witness to all the proceedings of the decades-long conflict. Marches, protests, rallies, sit-ins—its 360-degree gaze had stored and preserved the good and the bad times within its four walls since 1947.

Many statesmen had made passionate appeals here while delivering their speeches. It was at the

Ghanta Ghar that India's first Prime Minister Pandit Jawaharlal Nehru unfurled the national flag. It is also the stage from where he promised the right to self-determination for Kashmiris to choose the future of the state.

It was the same place where Sheikh Abdullah expressed his love for his friend, Pandit Nehru, using Amir Khusrau's Persian idiom:

> *Mann tu shudam, tu mann shudi*
> *Mann tann shudam, tu jan shudi*
> *Ta kas na goyad baad azee'in, mann digaram, tu digari.*
> ('I have become you, and you me,
> I the body, and you are my soul
> So. no one can say we are separate.')

Politicians would get the walls of the Clock Tower painted every now and then; while protesters threw stones at it. It had become a symbol of both resilience as well as deceit. Sponsors fought over replacing its clocks when the previous ones became defunct. It stood tall, erect. Barbed razor wires were strung around it to guard it. Round and round, they enveloped its exterior.

Like a watchful spectator, the tower saw

the changing political system of the valley, the fluctuating bureaucracy, the increasing traffic and generations of lovers walking hand in hand. Dwindling tourist visits and the rusted traffic lights. Heritage buildings being razed to the ground and plush markets taking their place. Gunshots, grenade attacks, pellet injuries, tear gas shells being hurled at protesters. If the valley ever needed to trace its history, it could go back in time by rewinding the broken hands of this magnanimous clock.

The shabby interiors of the Ghanta Ghar were a symbol of the shabby ambitions of its manipulators. Of late, protest calls to unfurl different flags on the tower top had become the order of the day.

That very afternoon Samar was savouring a Kashmiri wazwaan with Rabiya at Ahdoos restaurant. They now didn't mind being seen together in public. Just as they were about to finish the lavish meal, he received a call from his father who told him to return home as the situation in the city was worsening. He also told him about Mubarak's injury. Samar reluctantly told Rabiya that they should be heading home, before their areas could be put under the curfew. The two left at once in Samar's car. He dropped Rabiya near the street leading to her home. As he turned away from her house, he saw a huge crowd that had assembled in the area. He could hear the wailing and cries of women from a distance, and shots fired by policemen punctuating the voices of protesters.

As the tear gas shells became more frequent and the sound of the protests louder, he navigated the narrow lanes of downtown to reach home safely. Later in the evening, Samar went to see Mubarak. Naziya had applied an ice pack to his wounds and the blood oozing through the cotton bandage had dried up. Without disturbing Mubarak, Samar watched him through the old khatamband door open between the drawing room and the kitchen, where Mubarak was resting his injured forehead.

While Srinagar was burning, Pintoji was standing outside Sheikh Manzil and asking for a coin from a hurrying passer-by, who reached into his deep pheran pockets and took out some coins to hand them over to Pintoji.

'Mast moula, keep all the coins,' the passer-by told Pintoji.

Whenever a guest visited the Sheikhs, it seemed like Pintoji could sniff them and he would be seen loitering around the house. He sometimes accompanied the guests looking for the family or the metal shop in order to ensure they reached the right address. He would not enter the house. Through the jaali of the outer door, he would always say salaam to Naziya before going about his business. Pintoji was an eager helping hand in the neighbourhood. Sometimes he would insist on carrying the grocery and other household items all the way from Lal Chowk on his bicycle to Samar's house whenever he saw Shakeel Mirza shopping in the market. He would often be seen at the main gate of the Sheikhs, staring for hours at the courtyard, which harboured the canopy of green leaves and bunches of black and green grapes like chandeliers.

Pintoji would ambush Sana when she returned from school, snatch her schoolbag and Sana would have to chase him down the street. Pintoji took great pleasure in doing everything he had missed doing as a child. He had not received conventional education. He never went to school. Many schools denied him admission because he did not conform to what they thought was normal.

'Get him enrolled at one of those special schools,' one school principal told his foster parents. He had conveniently forgotten that there were no schools in the valley which could cater to the needs of differently abled children. It was then that his father decided that Pinto would study at home. During that phase of his life, Pinto had disappeared from the lanes of downtown for a long time. He wouldn't be seen in the streets during daytime. He would be seen only after dusk, all by himself when the stray dogs would bark at his shadow in the moonlight.

It was after a long time and sustained effort put in by his father that he started venturing out again, and this time he was more social. After rigorous screening, he was allowed to sit for his board exams. His days at the higher secondary school also passed somewhat peacefully. He was used to bullying; he had faced it in his neighbourhood. So he found it easier to deal with the bullies in school.

He managed to complete his higher secondary school studies with satisfactory results, which came as shock and surprise to many. It brought tears to his father's eyes, who had tutored him, shielded him and at times fought for him. He was a proud parent and he believed Pintoji would have a better future.

Meanwhile, Pinto's experiments with the spider in the toilet continued. One morning he saw the spider hanging from a thread in the washroom. He took the toilet brush and touched its bristles to the thread that the creature was hanging from. The thread got entangled in the bristles and the spider fell. It ran, limping on the tiles and disappeared. By afternoon, the spider was surprisingly hanging on to the thread again.

The little tease of a spider turned into an obsession for Pinto now. Each day he would go to the washroom to greet the spider, usually in the mornings. Every time Pinto pulled the chain down to flush, the creature obliged him with its gymnastic talent. Pinto would watch its movements intently. Like an ambitious research project, he discovered that it was normal for the spider to lean from the thin thread in search of insects and a bit of water. Pinto was convinced that the spider had some magical powers. He was meant to be his companion.

'Abbajaaan, did you notice the spider in our washroom?' Pinto asked his father, who was doing the office accounts, one evening.

Saying, 'No, I didn't see anything. Now let me do my work,' he shrugged him off and started his calculations all over again. His father had confirmed Pinto's belief. The spider was all his.

The next day, when purple clouds engulfed the sky and crows thronged over the houses in celebratory flights, Sana was keeping watch on their calf. Mubarak had brought it out to feed on khaj fal, some special fodder, that had accidently dropped on the roadside from a lorry as its driver rammed it into an electricity pole near the tomb. Seeing the calf chomping and relishing the feast, Sana herself felt hunger pangs.

Pinto saw Sana from a distance and started boasting about the spider to her over the fence. 'I have cast a spell on a spider, it now has magical powers,' he bragged.

'What nonsense, Pintoji. You can't cast a spell on anyone, forget a spider,' Sana casually rebuked him.

Sana's refusal to believe him angered Pinto. 'Okay, come. See for yourself,' he said. Sana agreed to go on the condition that Pinto would give her a chocolate. He agreed and guided Sana to the spider's abode.

The spider was hanging on the thread as usual. 'Filthy creature, thy master is here, get down and greet thy merciful Lord,' Pintoji said in a commanding voice. He had picked up some impressive-sounding lines from a Shakespeare play the neighbourhood children had been reciting. The spider, however, was quite unaffected and did not budge. Pinto was angry at being disobeyed. 'Shooo, come down you,' Pinto tried again.

The spider was adamant.

Sana was bored. 'I am going now. I knew you were lying,' she said and left before he could say anything.

Pintoji was angry. He should teach the spider a lesson, he thought. He collected some water in a hand-mug and splashed it on the spider. Nothing happened. He did it again. The thread tore apart and the spider fell on the floor. The turbulent water stream engulfed the spider into its waves. Pinto knew the spider was gone. It whirlpooled into the drain and then into a black tunnel.

16. WINTER CROWS

IN A CITY by the foothills of the Himalayas, where the sky changes from pink to magenta to bright white, there was no foreshadowing of the fate of two people passionately in love with each other. Samar and Rabiya, who came from two politically opposed families, had fallen in love. It was not love at first sight for Rabiya but one that grew over time. Books were shared, promises were made, and a hope lived through each other. Rabiya's dainty hands, the shape of her lips, her teasing smile—every move of hers was irresistibly attractive to Samar. His unflagging commitment and his resolve to fight the world for her was as clear to her as daylight.

Their final semester exams were over, both had been apprehensive about discussing life after their law degree. The two had never seriously thought about a time when they would have to face a situation where meeting each other would become a luxury. As they wrote their final exams, it was agreed upon that both would study further, even if that meant going out of the valley. But the biggest hurdle was Rabiya's father, Hilal, who was opposed to her leaving the valley. Salem Apa hadn't received a positive response from Rabiya's family either. Rabiya's father was well aware of her liking for Samar, but his political views were dearer to him than his daughter's wishes.

'What do you want to achieve now? Don't you see what happens to women outside the valley?' he would say.

'You can always join the court here. It won't be unbecoming of a woman if you do that,' her mother said.

'No need to go there either. I have seen what

lawyers do in court—haggle for people who come to the court for petty sums. Start a private practice. At least that way you could help our fellow Kashmiris fighting false cases.'

But every conversation would end in Hilal leaving the drawing room in a rage Rabiya had never known he was capable of.

~

Rosaline returned to New York. Past the vast oceans and amidst the uncertain nine clouds still hanging over her relationship with Douglas. Her husband was waiting at the airport. They drove back home in their black Ford sedan. Rosaline felt a change in the air, something different from what she had left behind. The weather was pleasant; the warm night air caressed her face. Douglas opened the door of their apartment on the thirty-second floor of the building.

The building stood taller than the nearby Mendocino tree. Everything was perfect, except her relationship with Douglas, but neither of them wanted to admit it. They hugged, pretending they had missed each other's company. At that moment, their bodies did touch but their souls stood miles apart. Soulmates...people had called them when they took their wedding wows.

~

Mubarak was sitting on a heap of timber wood shavings that had collected in front of his workshop. He was thinking about Rosaline. Was there a chance she would visit him again? He would ask Haleem how long had it been since Rosaline was gone even though he knew the answer. Something was amiss ever since she had left. He watched the black clouds gathering over his workshop. He was distracted as the dark clouds merged into a thunderous roar. Black smoke was spewing from the chimney over the metal shop. He watched it travel high up in the sky as it merged with the clouds. He thought at that moment that if he could possess the powers of that smoke, he could flow unhindered, as high as he wished to. As the surroundings became pitch dark, the rain came down to wash him of worldly desires; and ignoring the calls of his workers, he walked out into the rain.

'All is good as long as you don't fall ill in this rain. Oh lost soul! I don't want you to lose on a day's work. But another curfew has been announced today,' Naziya shouted from the window, pointing towards Haleem who was seeking Mubarak's approval for a new copper samovar design. He was polishing one on the lathe. Haleem had a permanent smile, and Mubarak a demoralized expression.

Amidst the incessant droning of crickets, Mubarak went inside the metal shop, and Naziya came with a cup of noun chai for Mubarak. No milkless kahwa anymore. The new cow was healthy and productive too. Sana, who had done well in her annual school exams, was also standing there, staring in confusion at her father.

~

As her parents' disapproval kept Rabiya and Samar away from each other, the absence of communication channels due to a curfew ensured an uneasy cooling of their relationship. They hadn't been able to see each other for a long time. The day before Samar was to leave for Delhi, the evening bulletins—the only way of receiving news from outside—announced the possibility of the network being restored by midnight.

Samar hurriedly sat down at his study table, dimmed the lights of the room, and helplessly started putting down his thoughts for Rabiya. He thought of pouring his heart out through an email before a phonecall in case the lines started working. He wrote many drafts. He wanted it to be perfect: 'It's been days since I have heard from you. I tried to meet you but the curfew has dashed my hopes so far. As I leave for the unforgiving plains tomorrow, I am writing to assure you of my love for you. I want you to believe in me, in us. I know our paths are separating, but our hearts yearn for the same thing—to be with each other. I want this to work despite the distance. I hope you are in this with me, by my side, My Love.'

Samar felt like it was the longest night of his life. Seeing a few towers pop on his internet connection, he happily pushed the 'send' button. After waiting anxiously for an hour, he realized that the email had remained unsent. Internet service had been snapped again after being briefly restored in some areas of the city. Calls to Rabiya's phone didn't get through either. There was no way to assure Rabiya of his love for her.

Rabiya, the more pragmatic of the two, had realized by now that the relationship wouldn't last without the permission of her family. Although she kept an eye on her network-starved cell phone, waiting for it to ring, she started drowning in the deafening calm of the night before she slid into sleep, numb and pale, dreaming of a world beyond the lofty mountains of the valley, where she lived happily with Samar.

The next morning, Samar looked reluctantly at his packed stuff. He had made the most difficult choice of his life—between his career and his heart. His father was adamant that he pursues a higher degree in law in Delhi. On this cold December morning, Samar picked up his luggage as his father accompanied him to Lal Chowk, where cabs were waiting to ferry passengers.

Pheran-clad drivers with all types of cabs, ranging from the common Tata Sumo and Mahindra Scorpio to the luxurious Tata Safari, thronged towards them.

'Jammu, Jammu, Jammu,' the agents were calling in their shrill, habitual tones, steam coming from their mouths like that of an engine.

Samar negotiated a front seat with a quiet-looking driver of a Tata Safari for five hundred rupees. He wanted to be on his own and did not want to be bothered during the journey.

As the cab was preparing to leave the taxi stand, for the first time Samar felt like his heart and mind had ventured on two separate journeys.

Shakeel Mirza was watching from a distance, waiting at the edge of the road near the fruit vendor, occasionally warming his hands, and then folding his arms to break the shackles of the freezing cold. He went up to Samar and handed over a wad of cash to him.

'Ten thousand more, count them once.'

'I have enough money, I won't need more this month. And If I need more, I can ask Adnan!'

'Keep it, you never know. If you don't spend it, I will send less next month. And don't keep it in the back pocket, it's not safe there,' Shakeel Mirza told him after which Samar slipped the money into his jacket pocket.

As the driver started to warm the engine of the vehicle, Shakeel Mirza turned to him again.

'Did you remember to carry your Identity Card?' he asked Samar, as he handed him the day's newspaper and a bottle of water, and gently touched his head.

The taxi left the stand amidst a flood of emotions and a flutter of pigeons. Just then a message popped on his new smartphone. It read: 'If something can't be taken to its logical conclusion, it's better to leave it on a beautiful note. By the way, Abbaji has fixed my marriage with a distant relative who works in Jeddah. He will be here next month for the nikaah. Wish you all the best.'

~

On the first day of chilai kalan, Pintoji looked at ease on his customary street ride. Pintoji had a vintage Atlas cycle which he rode through the narrow bylanes of downtown, or around the bund and the foreshore road around the Dal Lake. His bushy eyebrows rose up and his cheeks would puff up when he would cycle. The cycle's spokes had colourful bearings which formed a rainbow as the wheels turned. It had a fancy fan on the front mudguard and dazzling battery-powered lights.

Sana was watering the young chinar sapling in her courtyard, which had become dry like a snake molt. She watched Pintoji cycle away. Two dogs were following him and barking at him as if they had spotted a threat. Sana called out for him, but Pinto wasn't listening. Sana's gaze was fixed on him until he turned at the corner of the street. As Sana turned her attention back to the chinar sapling, a loud gunshot rang in the air. In no time, a large flock of winter crows hovered over the skies near Sheikh Manzil. Naziya rushed out in to the garden, grabbed Sana and took her inside, shutting the door behind her.